THE
SEAFARER

THE
SEAFARER

CONOR MCPHERSON

THEATRE COMMUNICATIONS GROUP
NEW YORK
2007

The Seafarer is published by Theatre Communications Group, Inc., 520 Eighth Avenue, 24th Floor, New York, NY 10018-4156

The Seafarer is published in arrangement with Nick Hern Books Limited, 14 Larden Road, London, England, W3 7ST.

This publication is made possible in part with public funds from the New York State Council on the Arts, a State Agency.

TCG books are exclusively distributed to the book trade by Consortium Book Sales and Distribution, 1045 Westgate Dr., St. Paul, MN 55114.

LIBRARY OF CONGRESS CATALOGING-IN-PUBLICATION DATA

McPherson, Conor.
The seafarer / by Conor McPherson.—1st ed.
p. cm.
ISBN 978-1-55936-312-9
I. Title.
PR6063.C73S43   2007
822'.914—dc22   2007040612

Cover design by Serino Coyne
Book design and composition by Lisa Govan

First Edition, November 2007

For Loolers,

the sun at Newgrange with love

THE
SEAFARER

The Seafarer was first performed in the Cottesloe auditorium of the National Theatre in London on September 28, 2006. The director was Conor McPherson, the designer was Rae Smith, the lighting designer was Neil Austin and the sound designer was Matthew Smethurst-Evans. The cast was:

JAMES "SHARKY" HARKIN	Karl Johnson
RICHARD HARKIN	Jim Norton
IVAN CURRY	Conleth Hill
NICKY GIBLIN	Michael McElhatton
MR. LOCKHART	Ron Cook

The Seafarer opened on Broadway at the Booth Theatre on October 31, 2007, with the same artistic team. The cast was:

JAMES "SHARKY" HARKIN	David Morse
RICHARD HARKIN	Jim Norton
IVAN CURRY	Conleth Hill
NICKY GIBLIN	Sean Mahon
MR. LOCKHART	Ciaran Hinds

TIME AND PLACE

The action takes place in a house in Baldoyle, a coastal settlement,
North Dublin. It is an old area which could hardly be called a town
these days. It is rather a suburb of the city with a church and a few
pubs and shops at its heart. From the coast here one is looking at
the north side of the Howth peninsula. Howth Head (Binn Eadair)
is a hill on the peninsula which marks the northern arm of Dublin
Bay. Due to its prominence it has long been the focus of myths and
legends.

Act One takes place on Christmas Eve morning and late afternoon. Act Two takes place late on Christmas Eve night.

Beware! Beware!
His flashing eyes, his floating hair!
Weave a circle round him thrice,
And close your eyes with holy dread,
For he on honey-dew hath fed,
And drunk the milk of paradise.

—SAMUEL TAYLOR COLERIDGE
Kubla Khan, 1797

He knows not
Who lives most easily on land, how I
Have spent my winter on the ice-cold sea
Wretched and anxious, in the paths of exile
Lacking dear friends, hung round by icicles
While hail flew past in showers . . .

—ANONYMOUS
The Seafarer, c. 755 A.D.,
translated from the Anglo Saxon
by Richard Hamer

ACT ONE

THE DEVIL AT BINN EADAIR

SCENE 1

The grim living area of a house in Baldoyle, North Dublin. The main entrance is down a flight of stairs from the ground floor, giving a basement feel to the room. Off the living area, there is a door going out to a small kitchen which allows access to a backyard. There is a toilet out that way too. There is a window with a net curtain and threadbare heavier curtains drawn over it. There is a stove, currently cold.

The place lacks a woman's touch. It has morphed into a kind of bar in its appearance. Those who live or pass through here are so immersed in pub culture that many artifacts in the room are originally from bars: a big mirror advertising whiskey, ashtrays, beer mats, a bar stool or two somewhere. The furniture is old and worn: an armchair, a couch, a little table more suited for playing cards than for eating, some chairs, etc.

As the play begins, the room is more or less in darkness. Some light seeps in through from the kitchen, from down the stairs (perhaps a window on the way up the staircase?), and through the threadbare curtains. There doesn't appear to be anyone here. A scrawny artificial Christmas tree haunts one corner.

Sharky comes downstairs, pausing to tap the red light under a picture of the Sacred Heart which has gone out. It flickers to life for a second, but goes out again as he descends and surveys the scene. He is in mismatched pajamas with a sweater over them and wears a pair of sneakers. He is not a big man, but is wiry and strong. A very tough life is etched on his face. His eyes are quick and ready. He has a small plaster at the bridge of his nose and a few plasters on the knuckles of his right hand. He opens the curtains to allow in the morning light, which reveals the squalor.

As he does so, Richard, his older brother, stirs awake. He has been asleep (passed out) on the floor where we didn't notice him (or took him for a bundle of rags). He wears a black suit, one slipper and a filthy white shirt. He is unshaven and looks terrible. He has recently gone blind.

RICHARD: Who's that? Sharky?

SHARKY *(Startled)*: What are you fucking doing?!

RICHARD: What happened?

SHARKY: Nothing—I just turned off the telly. I thought you told me you'd go up to bed!

RICHARD: Yeah, I meant to, but I'd no one to help me up the stairs!

SHARKY: Where was Ivan?

RICHARD: I don't know! He must've gone home. Give me a hand!

(Sharky helps Richard up.)

SHARKY: I thought you said you could feel your way up!

RICHARD: Ah, Sharky! Not when I'm jarred!

SHARKY *(Getting Richard to his feet, where he holds on to a chair)*: For fuck's sake, Richard . . .

RICHARD: Ah, don't be at me now, I'm not able for it. What time is it?

SHARKY: It's half ten.

RICHARD: Oh God, I'm bursting . . . give us a hand, where's me stick?

(Sharky looks around for Richard's stick, going over and peeping into the kitchen, while Richard shakily holds on to the armchair, one slipper on, one slipper off.)

Sharky!

SHARKY: I'm here.

RICHARD: God it's freezing! Where's me stick?

SHARKY: I don't know! Where did you put it?

RICHARD: If I knew where I put it, I'd have it!

SHARKY: Ah, don't fucking start, I'm looking for it, if you'd've let me bring you up to bed last night you'd have everything . . .

RICHARD: Ivan was here! What was I gonna do, leave him sitting in here on his own?

SHARKY: No, you were too busy drinking your fucking brains out.

(Sharky goes into the kitchen.)

RICHARD: Hark at you! Hark at Sharky! That's a good one! "The hypocrite's voice haunts his own den!"

(Sharky returns with the stick.)

SHARKY: Here I have it.

RICHARD: Where was it?

SHARKY: It was beside the downstairs jacks door. Where it was yesterday as well.

(Sharky gives Richard the stick and picks up the missing slipper, bringing it to Richard.)

RICHARD: Would you give me a hand and bring me through!!

SHARKY: I am! What do you think I'm doing?

(Sharky lifts Richard's stinking foot into his slipper.)

RICHARD: All right! I'm just asking . . . Jaysus, who got out of bed on the wrong side this morning?

SHARKY *(Helping Richard toward the kitchen)*: Good fuck, Richard, you absolutely stink again, do you know that?

RICHARD: Yeah, happy Christmas to you as well!

SHARKY: Would you not let me put you in the bath?

RICHARD: I told you! Tomorrow! Christmas morning! What's the point doing it today? I'll only stink the place out for Santy!

SHARKY: All right! Relax! You have me going deaf in that ear!

(They go into the toilet off the kitchen.)

(Off) Ah, Richard, who did that all over the floor?

RICHARD *(Off)*: Well I don't know!

SHARKY *(Off)*: Come on, let me bring you upstairs I'll give you a nice shave.

RICHARD *(Off)*: I said tomorrow! Would you let me do my toilet please, Sharky? For . . . Jaysus' sake will you come out of me road?

SHARKY *(Off)*: I am! Let me just wipe the seat . . .

RICHARD *(Off)*: Come out of me road!

(The toilet door slams. Sharky reappears and goes to the stove. He pokes around in there. He tidies up a few things, finding a bottle of Powers whiskey under a chair with about a quarter left, and brings it into the kitchen. As he reappears:)

(Off) Sharky!

SHARKY: What?

RICHARD *(Off)*: Is there not any jacks roll in here?

SHARKY: I don't know! You're in there!

RICHARD *(Off)*: Well there's none on the holder and I can't feel on the floor . . .

SHARKY: Hold on!

(Sharky goes into the kitchen.)

RICHARD *(Off)*: Don't come in!

SHARKY *(Off)*: Well what do you want me to do?

RICHARD *(Off)*: Just hand me in some!

SHARKY *(Off)*: There's only kitchen roll here, okay?

RICHARD *(Off)*: Just hand it in to me.

SHARKY *(Off)*: Here . . .

RICHARD *(Off)*: Where's your hand?

SHARKY *(Off)*: Here! Here!

(Sharky slams the toilet door.)

RICHARD *(Off)*: Don't slam the door!

(Sharky reappears and begins laying the table for some breakfast. He brings out a bowl of mandarin oranges, then a tray with some bowls and a Kellogg's Variety Pak. He goes back into the kitchen. Ivan appears at the top of the stairs. He is a big burly man with a red face and curly hair. He wears a shirt tucked into his pants, the back sticking out. He feels his way gingerly down.)

IVAN *(Sheepishly)*: Morning, Sharky.

SHARKY: Ivan! Did you stay over?

IVAN: Yeah, no I couldn't get a taxi. *(Hands shaking)* Oh God, I feel terrible.

SHARKY: Have some breakfast.

IVAN: Oh God, I don't know. Let me just . . . get my bearings for a minute, is that okay?

SHARKY: You don't have to ask me that, Ivan. Sure do whatever you—

IVAN: Yeah, no I . . . can't find my glasses. You didn't see them?

SHARKY *(Looking)*: Em . . . Where did you . . . did you get a good kip?

IVAN: Yeah, yeah . . . I was dead to the world just then. What was all the shouting?

SHARKY: Ah, that was . . . *(Signals "Richard")*

IVAN: When did you get back?

SHARKY: Three, four days ago.

IVAN: Yeah?

SHARKY: Sure I was talking to you last night!

IVAN: Were you here last night?

SHARKY: Yeah, I made yous hot whiskeys . . .

IVAN: Oh yeah . . .

SHARKY: Do you not remember?

IVAN: No, yeah, no, no I do. Just I wasn't even . . . sure I was only on my way home. I was only calling in to see if your man was all right . . . I certainly didn't mean to fucking still be here!

SHARKY *(Laughs)*: Yeah . . . yeah thanks for all the . . . calling in on him . . . he's . . . eh . . .

IVAN: Yeah, yeah, no, no bother. God I'm gonna be killed . . .

SHARKY: Are you?

IVAN: No there's still a few Christmas bits I have to do. God I'm gonna be killed now.

SHARKY: How is Karen keeping?

IVAN: Don't talk to me.

SHARKY: Yeah?

IVAN: Don't talk to me.

SHARKY: And the kids?

IVAN: Ah, they're great yeah. They're grand, you know yourself.

SHARKY: Yeah, well that's . . .

IVAN: Yeah . . .

(Pause.)

SHARKY *(Calling off)*: Are you all right there, Rich?

RICHARD *(Off)*: What's wrong with ya?

SHARKY *(Calling off)*: No, I was just seeing if you were all right?

RICHARD *(Off)*: Would you leave me alone? I'm trying to go to the fucking toilet in here!

SHARKY: I'll just grab the . . . the tea . . .

IVAN: Yeah work away.

(Sharky goes into the kitchen. Ivan moves through the room a little, throwing his eyes around quickly for something to drink. He can't see anything. Sharky comes back with a pot of tea and some milk.)

SHARKY: Here, were yous out the back last night?

IVAN: What? Oh! Yeah . . . Oh no it was . . . Did you hear him?

SHARKY: Ah yeah, I heard him, I heard yous. I rolled over, I tried to just ignore it. Sure that's . . .

IVAN: Yeah . . .

SHARKY: . . . that's a regular . . .

IVAN: I know, mad!

SHARKY: What was it? The winos out in the lane?

IVAN: Yeah! We were sitting there at the fire and bang! Suddenly he gets up! I'm like, "What are you doing?" He's like, "Them winos are out in the lane again! I'm gonna kill them!" he says, waving the fucking . . . stick around!

SHARKY: I know!

IVAN: Nearly took my fucking head off with it, and out he runs, off on out through the back there, it was nearly like he could see! You know?

SHARKY: I know!

IVAN: And I . . . fucking went over, smack! . . . on them newspapers all in the back door there, trying to stop him! And then out in the garden! I didn't know where I was!

SHARKY: I know. He's a mad bollocks, Ivan.

IVAN: Ah, he's all right. He's just ... So, here, did I ask you this last night? How did you get on down in ... Where was this you were?

SHARKY: I was down in Lahinch, in County Clare.

IVAN: Yeah?

SHARKY: Yeah, it was, it was, it was ... it was great.

IVAN: You got on well?

SHARKY: Yeah, got on great. Down the country is great, you know ...

IVAN: Ah, down the country's smashing. Were you on the boats?

SHARKY: Nah ... Can't get a job on the boats. But the people I was working for were spot on ...

IVAN: What were you doing? Chauffeur?

SHARKY: Yeah I was doing a bit of driving for this developer guy ... and his wife there and eh ... *(Short pause)* But I had to get back up because ... *(Signals "Richard")*

(They hear an attempt to flush the toilet.)

IVAN: Ah yeah, no, fair play, Sharky. Oh here, Nicky Giblin was telling me, how's the ...

(They stop to listen to Richard's attempts to flush the toilet.)

SHARKY *(Calling off)*: Are you all right, Rich?

RICHARD *(Off)*: Ah, I can't flush this fucking thing!

SHARKY *(Calling off)*: Do you want me to do it?

RICHARD *(Off)*: Is that Ivan out there?

SHARKY: He's heard you.

IVAN *(Going toward the kitchen door)*: Are you all right, Richard? Do you not want your brother?

RICHARD *(Off)*: No, Ivan, you're strong. Come here and give this yoke a yank, will ya?

(Ivan goes off to help Richard. Sharky continues to prepare the breakfast, bringing out some brown bread and butter while Ivan and Richard attempt to flush the toilet.)

(Off) That's it—one more like that, Ivan . . .

IVAN *(Off)*: Here give us that till I stick it down the . . . hold on, come away . . .

(The toilet flushes. Ivan leads Richard back out.)

RICHARD: Well done, Ivan . . . sorry about that . . .

SHARKY: Lads, some breakfast.

IVAN *(Unable to consider it)*: Oh . . .

RICHARD: What is there?

SHARKY: There's toast, if you want, there's cereal . . .

RICHARD: What cereal?

SHARKY *(Looking at the Variety Pak)*: There's Corn Flakes, there's Frosties, there's Coco Pops, there's . . .

RICHARD *(Gravely)*: Em . . . Coco Pops . . .

SHARKY: Okay, and I've mandarin oranges, there's tea, Ivan.

RICHARD: Did you not get coffee?

SHARKY *(Pouring out a bowl of cereal)*: No I told you, I forgot, I'll get it today.

RICHARD: You know what I'd really like?

SHARKY: What?

RICHARD: Ivan? Irish coffee . . .

IVAN: Oh now . . .

SHARKY: Yeah, well we don't even have coffee, so . . .

RICHARD: Well then we'll just have the Irish and no coffee—ha, Ivan?

SHARKY *(Going to the kitchen)*: I'll put on some toast.

RICHARD: Well, Ivan, how's the head?

IVAN: Don't talk to me, Rich. I can't find my glasses. I'm like you, I'm feeling my way around.

RICHARD: Well they have to be here somewhere. Did you have them when you got here?

IVAN: I'm assuming I did.

(Sharky comes back.)

RICHARD *(Referring to Sharky)*: Hey, check out Johnny Weiss-muller, off the drink for . . . what is it, Sharky? Two days?

SHARKY: What?

RICHARD: How long are you on the dry now? Two days is it? I was just telling Ivan.

(Sharky ignores him.)

IVAN: Yeah, well fair play. Hey, Shark, I was gonna ask you, how's the nose? Nicky Giblin was telling me.

(Sharky signals to him not to continue with this line of inquiry. Ivan doesn't twig it in time.)

RICHARD: What's this?

IVAN: Did he not tell you?

SHARKY *(Signaling to Ivan, who finally sees him)*: No, it was nothing . . .

RICHARD: Tell me what?

(Pause.)

What? Tell me what?

IVAN: No . . . eh . . . Nicky was . . . *(Dismissively)* Ah, you know Nicky . . .

RICHARD: I know Nicky well! What happened to you, Sharky?

SHARKY: Ah, it was nothing, it was . . .

RICHARD: What? Ivan?

IVAN: Ah . . . *(To Sharky)* Nicky was saying, I was only asking to see if you were . . . *(To Richard)* Nicky was saying that Sharky got in a spot of bother there off someone there outside the Elphin and I was just . . .

RICHARD: When was this?

SHARKY: Ah, it was . . . it was the other evening . . . the night I got here.

RICHARD: You kept that very quiet! What happened?

SHARKY: Ah, it was fucking . . . I got off the Dart at Howth Junction and I was . . .

RICHARD: What did you get off at Howth Junction for?

SHARKY: Ah, I meant to go to Bayside or Sutton Cross, and I mixed it up and I . . .

RICHARD: You blew it!

SHARKY: Yeah, well I was walking all up there, up the coast, and . . .

RICHARD: Why didn't you get a taxi?

SHARKY: I had no cash!

RICHARD: Go on out of that, you were in the Elphin!

SHARKY: No I went *into* the Elphin . . .

RICHARD *(Sarcastically, as though he had failed to see a big distinction)*: Oh!

SHARKY: I needed to make a phone call . . . my phone was . . .

RICHARD: Go on out of that! You were jarred from the train, you got off at the wrong station . . .

SHARKY: I fucking . . . ! I had two, *three* pints . . . *(To Ivan)* 'cause young Cathy Wolfe was having her birthday in there and her da bought me one . . .

RICHARD: Oh . . . I *see* . . .

SHARKY: And then the end of the match was on and . . .

RICHARD: Ah, of *course* . . .

SHARKY: Ah, I'm not gonna fucking tell you if you're . . .

RICHARD: No, I'm only having you on! What happened?

(Pause.)

SHARKY: Ah . . . I was coming out and there was some lads messing around, sitting on the bonnet of a car out there and . . .

(Pause.)

RICHARD: What happened?

SHARKY: Ah, I just said, "Come up off of that . . ." as I was kind of walking by . . .

RICHARD: What?

SHARKY: Just, only, not even that serious, you know . . .

RICHARD: You fucking eejit . . .

SHARKY: And next thing, I'm down at the corner, they're all around me! And your man is, "What did you fucking say?" And all this. And I'm like, "Ah, lads, I was only . . ." And then, one of them . . . he just gave me this *unbelievable* kick in the arse, you know? And it was so . . . it was so . . . the humiliation of it like, and I . . .

RICHARD: Ah, Sharky . . .

SHARKY: I turned around and I threw a dig and I was . . . but there was loads of them and I got an awful couple of smacks in the . . . my nose was pumping, it's all right now, but I had to leg it back into the Elphin. The fucking . . . streams of toilet roll I had stuck up my nose . . . it was so . . . The Wolfes put me in a cab, gave your man twenty euros to drop me up.

(Short pause.)

RICHARD: Why didn't you say anything? *(Short pause)* You fucking eejit!

SHARKY: Yeah, well, I'll get the toast.

(Sharky goes into the kitchen.)

IVAN: Mmm . . .

RICHARD: I mean, what can you do with a fella like that?

IVAN: Yeah it was . . . they were all . . . Nicky Giblin was telling me . . .

RICHARD: Yeah, well Nicky means well, I'm sure . . .

(Short pause.)

IVAN: Does Sharky know that Eileen is with Nicky now?

RICHARD: What? Ah yeah . . . no that's . . . Sure that's . . . she called into me here about two weeks ago, did I tell you that?

IVAN: Who, Eileen?

RICHARD: Yeah she was here, she does a morning or two cleaning for the Franciscans up there in the friary. She called in to see if I was . . . to see how I was. We had smoked cod and chips from the chipper and everything. Ah, it was great, we were talking about Head-the-Ball *(Referring to Sharky)* . . . and Nicky and . . . yeah, the whole . . .

IVAN: Ah, I'm kind of avoiding Nicky, to be honest with you, Dick.

SHARKY: Why?

IVAN: Ah, there's just always some fucking shite going on and I'm—

(Ivan clams up as Sharky returns with some toast.)

SHARKY: Can you see there, Ivan?

IVAN: I can just about . . .

SHARKY: Would you . . . *("help Richard")*

IVAN: Yeah, yeah, do you want some toast there, Dick?

(Ivan starts to very shakily butter some toast as Sharky nips back into the kitchen to get some for himself.)

RICHARD: I tell you what I'd love. I'd love a big Irish breakfast! A big fry with all white pudding and a runny egg and all . . .

(Sharky returns with his own toast.)

Do you hear me Sharky?

SHARKY: What?

RICHARD: We should be having a nice Christmassy breakfast. We have to get some decent grub in for tomorrow, Sharky. Christmas pud and the works. This is disgraceful!

SHARKY: Yeah, I'm going up now when I get dressed . . .

RICHARD: How will you go?

SHARKY: Do you have your car with you, Ivan?

(Pause. Ivan looks at him blankly.)

RICHARD: Do you have your car, Ivan?

IVAN: I'll tell yous, lads . . . I don't know.

RICHARD: We'll go in a taxi.

SHARKY: Are you coming as well?

RICHARD: Ah, let me get out for bit, for Jaysus' sake, Sharky, we might even get a Christmas pint . . .

SHARKY *(Sighs)*: Oh . . . well wait now because if—

RICHARD: No, because we need to get a few bits in as well, Sharky, from the off-license, in case anyone calls. We'll get a taxi back, because I want to be settled in here now for Christmas Eve . . .

SHARKY: Yeah, but if I have to—

RICHARD *(Sudden despair)*: I have so little left to live for!

(Pause.)

IVAN *(Reassuringly)*: Ah, now, Richard . . .

RICHARD: What?! Yous don't know. Yous don't know.

SHARKY: No we'll all . . . we'll all go . . . we'll get the few bits and . . .

IVAN: Sure you'll be grand, you'll have a grand Christmas here with Sharky here with you and all, and . . .

RICHARD *(Dismally)*: Yeah . . .

SHARKY: If we're going out . . . will you have a wash?

RICHARD *(Shouts)*: I'll have a wash tomorrow!! I told you! Now leave it!

(Pause.)

IVAN: God, I'll have to find my glasses. Karen'll kill me, God what am I gonna say?

SHARKY: We'll find them, I'll have a look now in a minute before we go.

IVAN: Thanks, Sharky.

SHARKY: Tea, Rich?

RICHARD *(Sheepishly)*: Yeah, thanks.

(Sharky brings him a cup of tea.)

I just don't want to be cooped up all over the . . .

SHARKY: Yeah, I know, we'll get out, we'll get you some fresh air.

RICHARD: Yeah . . .

IVAN: Hey, any sign of your money there yet, Sharky? From the bus people?

SHARKY: What? Aw . . . Well, the . . .

RICHARD: Get this!

SHARKY: Well, no, because the solicitor fucking . . . he misdated the statement I gave him. About the . . . the actual night I fell down the stairs . . .

IVAN: What, the bus went round the wrong corner, or a different corner or something, was it?

SHARKY: Yeah he went around the wrong corner up there at Christchurch there, he went around too early, and I was getting up to get off . . . but that's . . . no one is disputing that, but the date, you see on the . . . it's the wrong date and . . .

IVAN: Can you not just . . . ?

SHARKY: Nah, the courts are . . .

RICHARD: He put the wrong year on it!

SHARKY: The whole thing has been put right back now, I don't even know if . . .

IVAN: But can he not just change the . . .

RICHARD: It's a shambles . . .

IVAN: . . . the year . . .

SHARKY: No . . .

IVAN: . . . if it was just a mistake . . .

RICHARD: Ivan, the law . . . the law is the law. It has to be.

IVAN: Yeah . . .

SHARKY: So now I have to look at . . .

IVAN: Yeah, if you keep . . .

SHARKY: No, if I want to start the whole thing off again . . .

IVAN: What?

RICHARD: Yeah. Seven and a half years he's been . . .

SHARKY: Ah, it doesn't matter, it's too . . .

IVAN: Jaysus, that's a pain in the bollocks isn't it?

SHARKY: Ah, it's . . . (*Waves it away*)

IVAN: 'Cause I'd say you could've done with the few bob . . .

SHARKY: Yeah well . . .

IVAN: Nightmare . . .

RICHARD: Of course, he was using your man, that solicitor out of Kilbarrack.

SHARKY: Yeah, all right, Rich . . .

IVAN: That drinks in The Fox & Hound?!

RICHARD: Yeah, your man that does be falling around the car park!

SHARKY: Ah no, see it was him that . . .

RICHARD (*Shaking his head*): Sharky . . .

SHARKY: I was never even gonna take a case! It was him that . . . I mean . . .

RICHARD: What a shambles . . .

SHARKY: Yeah well . . .

IVAN: Aw well, I'm sorry to hear that, Shark. I only saw your man the other week there actually, and the Baker, and Steady Eddie and all them lads were down in Graingers. Do you know what they were talking about? Do you remember Maurice Macken?

RICHARD: That used drive the milk lorry?

IVAN: Yeah, and then he got into the electrical trade. Do you remember him, Sharky?

SHARKY: The skinny fella?

IVAN: Yeah, used play a lot of cards all up around Sutton and Howth you heard what happened him?

RICHARD: Oh yeah, I heard all about that.

SHARKY: Was this in the paper?

IVAN: Yeah it was all in the paper, you would've seen it. He was electrocuted up in a house where he was working in Santry. There was a tremendous bang! Blew him right across the room I believe. One of his fillings ended up in his ear. Somehow he survived. They let him go home out of Beaumont Hospital, and then there was a fire in his house that night! And he was gone!

RICHARD: Gobshite . . .

SHARKY: Jaysus that's mad.

IVAN: His number was up! His number was just up and he was going to have to go, one way or the other, you know what I mean, mad! Survived the electrocution only to be burned!

RICHARD: Fucking eejit . . .

IVAN: But listen, what the lads were saying up in Graingers—two people, two different people, now, saw Maurice Macken, after he was buried, hanging around at the off-license serving hatch round the side near the car park.

RICHARD *(Incredulous)*: Come on!

IVAN: Two different people saw him, Dick, on different nights. And apparently a barman tidying up after they were closed said he heard someone shouting in the jacks—and when he went in, there was no one there.

23

RICHARD: That's bollocks.

IVAN: Yeah, well apparently he looks really white. He was standing near the hatch. Big Bernard's cousin saw him. Apparently he was just standing there looking out into the car park, like he was waiting on a lift or something.

RICHARD: Go on out of that! What's he waiting on? A few cans? *(Laughs)*

IVAN *(To Sharky)*: Spooky though, isn't it?

SHARKY: Yeah well . . .

RICHARD *(Mild derision)*: Yeah, right . . .

(Suddenly there are three loud bangs at the front door upstairs. Richard jumps with fright.)

Fucking hell! Who's that?

SHARKY *(Going up the stairs)*: Probably the postman . . .

RICHARD: We have a letterbox! For the love of God . . .

(Short pause.)

IVAN *(Sighs)*: Yeah . . .

RICHARD: Ivan, quick, where did he put that Gold Label?

IVAN *(Quickly squinting around)*: I can't fucking see, Dick . . .

RICHARD: Have a look in the kitchen, go on quick.

(Ivan strides purposefully toward the kitchen.)

On top of the fridge or in the press with the pots . . .

(Ivan disappears into the kitchen and returns quickly with the bottle Sharky had put away earlier, unscrewing the lid.)

IVAN: Here, Rich, give us your cup.

RICHARD *(Offering his cup of tea to Ivan)*: Pour that out.

(Ivan takes Richard's cup and wildly looks for somewhere to pour it out, deciding eventually to pour it on to the carpet nearby, bending low so as not to make a splashing sound. He then rubs the steaming carpet with his foot and pours a big dollop of whiskey into Richard's cup, handing it to him. Richard raises it to his mouth immediately. Ivan goes to the table to look for a cup for himself, swigging a mouthful of whiskey from the neck of the bottle as he does so. He grabs a mug and pours some whiskey, wheeling around to give Richard another shot, as Richard instinctively holds his cup out for it. Both men retch and make faces as though their throats are burning. Their arms and legs undergo a rudimentary stretch as they seem to come alive. Ivan pours some tea on top of the whiskey in his cup and conceals the bottle when Sharky appears at the top of the stairs. Sharky descends with a tastefully gift-wrapped box.)

(Brightly) What was it, Shark?

SHARKY: Postman.

IVAN: Look at that!

RICHARD: What is it?

SHARKY: It's a . . . it's a present . . .

RICHARD: For who?

SHARKY: For me.

RICHARD: Who's it from?

SHARKY: Ah, the, the people I was working for down in Clare . . . His wife, Miriam, she's very . . . you know . . . *(To Ivan)* She's a very nice lady, she's eh . . .

RICHARD: Woooooooooo! *(Childishly)* The big birthday present!

SHARKY: It's a Christmas present, you dozy fucking eejit.

RICHARD: Oh! *(Same tone)* A Christmas present! Anything good?

SHARKY *(Handing Richard an envelope)*: Here, there's a card here for you.

RICHARD: Who's it from?

SHARKY: The Department of Social Welfare.

RICHARD *(Throwing it away)*: Ah, that's only my balls!

(Sharky opens the card that came with his present. He stands there reading it to himself. Ivan slurps his tea.)

Well? What is it?

(Sharky looks at him as though coming out of a daze.)

SHARKY: What?

IVAN: Are you gonna open it up?

RICHARD: Yes! Cheer us all up! Presents arriving for Sharky! What next?

(Sharky takes the wrapping off.)

What is it?

SHARKY: It's a few CDs.

IVAN: Nice one!

RICHARD *(Childishly)*: Wooooooo, music to put you in the mood! . . . For getting in your nude! . . .

IVAN: Hey, she knows her stuff! Some of these are classics! Here, put one on!

RICHARD: No! Later! We have to go and get the few bits for the Christmas! Come on . . .

IVAN: I have to find my glasses!

RICHARD: Sharky'll look for them. Sharky, have a quick look for Ivan's specs, will you?

SHARKY: Where would they be, Ivan? Where did you sleep?

IVAN: Eh, in the box room.

SHARKY: There's no bed in there!

IVAN: I slept on the rug.

SHARKY: The rug?

RICHARD: Ah, Ivan . . .

IVAN: Ah, no, there was towels, and there was . . .

SHARKY: I'll have a quick look. You should've slept in the spare room . . . *(Goes up the stairs)*

IVAN: Ah, no, I was grand, I was fine . . .

RICHARD: Did you just sleep on the floor?

IVAN: No I slept on the rug.

RICHARD: Ah, I don't even know what you're talking about. Give us a hand, Ivan, will you?

IVAN *(Helping Richard up)*: I thought Sharky was in the spare room.

RICHARD: I often just go off here at the fire. *(Coughs up some deeply embedded old phlegm and rubs it into the side of the armchair)* You should have got into my bed.

IVAN: Nah, I wouldn't do that, Dick. Here, do you want your shoes?

RICHARD: Ah, sure, we'll get a taxi, my slippers is grand. I don't expect we'll be walking the street like hoboes. Just get us my anorak hanging up there behind the kitchen door.

(Ivan goes to the kitchen. Richard feels around for his cup. Ivan brings Richard's anorak.)

Is that Gold Label dead? We have to make a list.

(Ivan finds his own coat, which he puts on. He goes to retrieve the bottle from whatever nook he hid it in. There is only a swig left.)

We have nothing organized. That's your man, of course. He was supposed to get up to me weeks ago. His head is arseways. You're seeing him on the dry now, that's why he's running around in here like a fly in a bottle. But of course then with jar on him he's worse! Throwing digs outside the Elphin? Or getting in mills outside the chipper on Kilbarrack Road the last time he was here! Getting arrested by the Guards up in Howth! I mean what am I going to do?

(As Ivan drains the last shot of whiskey . . .)

Here, is there a shot left in that Powers, Ivan?

IVAN: Nah, we've had it. Here do you want your anorak, Dick?

RICHARD *(Sighs heavily)*: Yeah . . .

(Ivan helps Richard put on his anorak.)

Here, if you're gonna be round tomorrow, you should drop in, do you know what I have that I've been saving? A drop of Brigid Blake's poteen, that Big Bernard got me . . .

IVAN: Oh, look out!

RICHARD: That'll fucking . . .

(He makes a high-pitched whistle, pointing to his head. Ivan laughs. Sharky descends down the stairs. He is now dressed and wears his coat.)

SHARKY: Ivan, I can't see your glasses anywhere.

RICHARD: Ah, they have to be somewhere, Sharky!

SHARKY: Do you not have a spare pair at home'll do you till . . . ?

IVAN: Yeah, I think I . . . they're an older prescription, if I can find them . . . Oh God, Karen is gonna kill me.

RICHARD: No, no she won't! I'll ring her, I'll say I had them here, it'll be grand. Sharky, get a pen. We need to make a list. Ivan, I expect we'll be seeing you over the Christmas, I'll be very disappointed if we didn't. So, Sharky, Harp, what, four six-packs?

SHARKY *(Grabbing a pen)*: Yeah, Harp . . .

IVAN: Ah, don't just do that for me, Rich. Sharky, I'll drink whatever's going.

RICHARD *(Pointing imperiously)*: No. Sharky.

SHARKY *(Writing this down)*: Yeah, Harp. Stout, Richard?

RICHARD: Yeah and Paddy Powers. Get three bottles.

SHARKY: Three bottles? The off-license is open again on Monday, Rich.

RICHARD: If we have visitors they may want a hot whiskey. It's called being festive. I know you may not comprehend it, Sharky, but some us like to be social. Ivan, Christmas? You *have* to!

IVAN: Ah, Christmas is great!

RICHARD: And Miller for Nicky.

SHARKY: For Nicky Giblin?

RICHARD: Nicky drinks Miller, Sharky. We all understand that you have issues with life and it's a struggle for you to grasp human relationships, but Nicky is a friend of mine. And a friend of Ivan's . . . and . . .

IVAN: Ah, he can be very messy, Richard.

RICHARD *(With finality)*: The man is welcome here!

SHARKY *(Writing)*: Bottles of Miller.

RICHARD: Thank you.

SHARKY: What'll I get for tomorrow? A chicken?

RICHARD: Turkey! Turkey!

SHARKY: We won't get a turkey now at this stage, Rich . . .

IVAN: Karen is doing us a big turkey tomorrow, I could drop down with maybe a few . . .

RICHARD: No, no, Ivan, we couldn't do that to you, we'll a get turkey, don't worry about it . . .

SHARKY *(Sucking his pen)*: I mean we might be able to get a piece of 'em . . .

RICHARD: Look! Let's go!

SHARKY: Do you not want to make a . . . ?

RICHARD: Yeah, yeah, we'll get all that when we're there. We'll see all that. Ivan, will you take me out the back way and we'll hail a taxi on the road? I want to check them awful fucking winos haven't been messing around at our laneway door.

(Ivan leads Richard out through the kitchen.)

Will you lock up, Sharky?

SHARKY: Yeah.

RICHARD: We'll see you out on the road. (*As they go*) All the kids' presents got then, Ivan?

IVAN: Ah, yeah . . .

RICHARD: Well, I hope so, says you!

> (*As they leave, Sharky folds up the list and puts it in his pocket. He takes out his keys and goes to the kitchen, locking the back door after them. He comes back into the silence and picks up the card. He looks at it for a moment, then briskly puts it in his pocket and leaves, running up the stairs.*
>
> *Music plays as the lights slowly change from bright morning to a dusky feel as we slide into:)*

SCENE 2

The wind is picking up outside as the sunlight fades and the temperature drops. The music dies away as Sharky comes down the stairs with bags of shopping—mostly from the off-license, which he takes into the kitchen. A church bell chimes solemnly somewhere off in the distance. He reappears and bends down under the scraggy old Christmas tree and plugs in some colored fairy lights. He sees two little wrapped presents there. He picks one up and looks at it for a moment, wondering about it, before he puts it back. He goes back up the stairs, pausing to tap the extinguished light under the Sacred Heart. It doesn't come on. He continues up the stairs to get the rest of the shopping. He reappears carrying more bags. As he descends, we hear Richard calling from off, upstairs in the hallway.

RICHARD (*Off*): What are you fucking doing?

SHARKY (*Halting and turning*): What?

RICHARD: What, are you gonna just leave me up here?

SHARKY: I thought you could manage your way down!

RICHARD: Ah, not when I'm jarred, Sharky!

SHARKY: Just give me a second.

(Sharky carries the bags down, leaving them at the bottom of the stairs, then makes his way back up.)

RICHARD *(Off)*: I'm freezing!

(Sharky reappears, helping Richard down.)

You are in one foul humor today . . .

SHARKY: Richard, now, please don't start . . .

RICHARD *(Warmly, paternally)*: Sit down, sit down. Sit down, sit down.

(They sit on the stairs.)

What's the matter with you?

SHARKY: I'm . . .

RICHARD: What . . .

SHARKY: Nothing's the matter with me.

(Richard stands, rubbing his hands. Sharky starts clearing a few things away, taking the breakfast things on a tray into the kitchen.)

RICHARD: God it's freezing! Would you get the fire going for the love of Jaysus, Shark?

SHARKY *(Off)*: I am! I'm doing it! I've a million things to do here, just give me a second, would you?

RICHARD *(As though Sharky has completely overreacted)*: Okay! Okay!

(Sharky returns, goes to the stove, puts some peat briquettes in and sets about lighting it.)

God, I never seen such a Christmas wrecker! Would you not have left the old Kaliber out for today and had a drink with me and Ivan . . . and . . .

SHARKY (*Working at the stove*): I'm pissed off with you, Richard.

RICHARD: With *me*? Why? What did I do now?

SHARKY: What did you have to go and invite Nicky Giblin up here for?

RICHARD: When?

SHARKY: When Big Bernard let you speak to him on his mobile.

RICHARD: Ah, that was only a Happy Christmas, Jimmy, come on . . .

SHARKY: You told him to call in to us . . .

RICHARD: But sure, that's what you say! That's what everybody says!

SHARKY: You told him to call in to play cards!

RICHARD: That's . . . that's just what you say! Anyway—so what?! Would you stop being such a curmudgeonly old bollocks your whole life, will you?

(Pause. Sharky works . . .)

(Warmly, drunkenly conciliatory) Ah, Sharky . . . I only said to stick the head in if he was in the area . . .

SHARKY: You don't fucking say that to fellas like Nicky, Dick. He'll be in on top of us before you know it!

RICHARD: No he won't! He was plastered! He was down in the Brookwood Inn of all places! How the hell is he gonna rock up here? In a taxi? I don't think so! Hey, is there 'ere a Christmas drink going a begging around here?

SHARKY: Yeah, well I saw him the other day, and he was driving *my* car, Richard.

RICHARD: Who?

SHARKY: Nicky Giblin!

RICHARD: Yeah, well you gave your car to Eileen!

SHARKY: I *loaned* it to her for the school run, Dick. I didn't ever expect to see that fucker driving around in it! I saw him pulling out of the shops down there in Bayside, and I was walking down to get the Dart in the pissing rain! And he was in *my* car!

RICHARD: Ah, grow up, Sharky! What do you want? Him and Eileen are together now, so get over it, 'cause that's life, okay? Now would you ever give us a Jaysus fucking drink, you're gonna blow the whole Christmas atmosphere. This is all I have! And how many do I have left? Maybe only this one! Maybe that's it for me!

SHARKY: What are you talking about?

RICHARD: Ah! It's hardly even worth it! . . . What's the point?

(Richard turns away in disgust. Sharky takes the rest of the shopping into the kitchen. Richard opens his coat and makes his way unsteadily toward the armchair and sits forlornly. Sharky reemerges with a glass of whiskey for him.)

SHARKY: Here . . . Richard . . .

RICHARD: What?

SHARKY *(Putting the drink in Richard's hand)*: Here . . .

RICHARD: Ah, thanks, Sharky.

(Sharky goes to the kitchen and comes back with a festive-looking candle in a red glass holder. He is tearing the price and the cellophane wrapping off as he brings it to the windowsill.)

What's that?

SHARKY: Hmm?

RICHARD: What are you doing, there?

SHARKY: Ah, I'm just gonna put an old candle in the window.

RICHARD: Ah, that's nice. That's more like it, Sharky. I never like it when you're down. It changes the whole . . .

SHARKY: Would you like some smoked salmon and brown bread?

RICHARD: Oh, now, that sounds . . . Ah, thanks, Sharky . . . thanks. Delicious!

SHARKY: Keep us going anyway . . . Is that getting warm?

RICHARD: Oh we're warming up now . . .

(Sharky goes toward the kitchen.)

Oh, Sharky. Just one . . . just one small thing, quickly, before you do that.

SHARKY: Yeah?

RICHARD: You wouldn't take a basin of hot water down out to the back door at the lane? . . . Them filthy fucking winos have all puke and piss and everything else all down our step all up the fucking door out there . . .

SHARKY *(Face dropping)*: Are you serious?

RICHARD: Ah, it's absolutely disgusting. We can't leave it like that on Christmas Eve . . . It'll only take you a minute . . . Good man . . .

(Sharky goes unhappily to the kitchen to boil the kettle. Richard cozily raises his shoulders as though he is snuggling down into a lovely warm bed.)

Now, this is nice now. It's getting nice and Christmassy now . . .

(There is a loud rapping at the front door upstairs. Richard turns toward it. Sharky steps back into the room.)

Sharky!

SHARKY: I hear it.

RICHARD: Well get it, will you!

SHARKY: I'm not gonna get it, I told you I don't want Nicky Giblin in here, I just don't want it.

RICHARD: What!?

(There are more loud raps at the door.)

SHARKY: I told you, Richard! Why do you have to do this to me?

RICHARD: What are you talking about? I'm not doing anything to you. Don't be a fucking child, will you, and get the door for God's sake . . .

(Sharky just stands there looking at Richard. Richard suddenly bursts up out of his chair.)

I'll get it myself!

(With surprising speed, Richard darts toward the staircase. He hits the wall, collapses, bounces up again, grabs the banister and attempts to pull himself up the stairs.)

SHARKY: Richard! Hold on, will you?

(Sharky runs across and grabs Richard. Richard stumbles and falls backward into Sharky's arms, the two of them sinking to the ground as the doorbell rings.)

RICHARD: What are you fucking doing?!

SHARKY: What are *you* fucking doing? Come back over here and sit down, will you?

(Sharky bundles Richard toward the armchair.)

For fuck's sake . . .

RICHARD: Will you get the door?

SHARKY: Yeah, will you just sit down please?

(Sharky storms angrily up the stairs. Richard gets up and feels around for his glass which has fallen somewhere. We hear Sharky's voice from upstairs.)

(Off) No, no, it's no problem! Don't be silly . . . come on, come on down to Richard.

IVAN *(Off)*: I'm sorry, Sharky.

(Sharky leads Ivan down.)

I'm sorry, Richard, I'm sorry to . . .

RICHARD: Who is it? Ivan?

IVAN: Richard, I'm sorry, I'm barging in on you again . . . I'm sorry, Sharky . . .

SHARKY: No . . .

RICHARD: What's the matter with you?

IVAN: Karen's after completely doing her nut.

RICHARD: What? Why?

IVAN: Ah, even if I . . . I should've just gone straight home, it might have been different. But after you left and I was gonna head, I was just standing outside Doyle's with Big Bernard having a smoke, she was coming out of the post office and I didn't have my glasses and I didn't see her and . . .

RICHARD: Did you not get your spare glasses?

IVAN: I didn't even get in the house, Dick! She fucking reefed me out of it! *(His face crumples in pain)* The kids were there and . . . *(A sudden impassioned plea)* I only went in to have that quick one with yous! I was on my way home! Yous know that! But sure then there was people buying me Christmas pints left and right—I couldn't even see who they were to say no! *(Sinks into a chair)* This is a disaster!

RICHARD: Ah, now, come on, Ivan . . .

IVAN: I hate it when the kids see us fighting and . . .

RICHARD: These things happen.

IVAN: Now I'm after ruining Christmas on them all again!

RICHARD: No you haven't! She'll calm down . . . Just take it easy . . . Sharky, where's your manners? Will you get poor Ivan something to drink?

SHARKY: I'll tell you what. I've a nice bit of smoked salmon we were gonna have, and there's little mince pies I was gonna heat up. Will you have one, Ivan?

IVAN *(Rubbing his face)*: Oh, I don't know . . .

SHARKY: Ah, it'll do you good, Ivan . . .

IVAN: I suppose . . . thanks, Sharky.

RICHARD: Yeah, great, and get him a drink, will you, Sharky? Good man.

(Sharky goes to the kitchen.)

Now, not to worry, Ivan. The woman is being completely unreasonable, she'll come round, just you watch. And we'll be nice and cozy here now and we'll figure it out . . .

(Sharky returns with some glasses, a can of Harp for Ivan, and a bottle of whiskey for Richard.)

Sharky, *(A little laugh)* I lost my drink in the . . . in the confusion there . . .

SHARKY: I have one here for you.

RICHARD: Ah, thanks. Hey, I know! Sharky'll go back up with you, Ivan.

(Sharky impotently shoots a look at Richard.)

Sharky, you'll explain! His glasses have to be here somewhere! And we can . . .

IVAN: Oh I don't know, I wouldn't go up there now at the moment, Sharky. She absolutely now . . . she fucking reefed me out of it. There was fucking people all standing there looking at us . . . even Bernard just went back in.

RICHARD: No, no, we'll let her cool down, absolutely . . .

(Sharky gives Ivan a glass of beer.)

IVAN: Thanks, Sharky.

RICHARD: Yeah, and get the mince pies, we'll get nice and Christmassy here now!

SHARKY: Yeah, I've the oven heating up.

RICHARD: Oh and listen, don't forget to wash that auld step and the door in the lane, will you?

SHARKY: Yeah, I'll do it . . .

RICHARD: Good man, Sharky.

(Sharky goes into the kitchen, then out the back door.)

(Raising his glass, brightly) Now! Happy Christmas!

IVAN: Yeah . . . happy Christmas . . .

RICHARD: Sure here we are, aren't we? Ha? We're having a nice Christmas drink. And we'll let the whole . . . Ivan, are you listening to me?

IVAN: Yeah. No, I am . . .

RICHARD: The whole situation will . . . *("settle down")* And we'll talk to her and . . . And we'll all be right as dodgers. Do you hear me?

IVAN: Yeah, I'm sorry, Richard.

RICHARD: No, no, no, no, no, no, no . . . She'd have been rid of you long ago at this stage if your marriage wasn't strong enough to weather a little bump every now and again . . . Come on! When I used clean windows all up along, all up the coast all up into Sutton, I saw every conceivable kind of men and women all shacked up in myriad . . . *(With sudden force)* myriad, states of confusion and banjacksed relationships, believe

me. You and Karen are just passionate people . . . and you're
. . . This is going to happen every now and again—not a big
deal! And if we can't shelter the weary traveler on Christmas
Eve of all nights sure what way would we . . .

*(The doorbell rings, a loud cutting sound. Ivan looks at Richard.
Pause.)*

(Calling) Sharky! *(Pause)* Ah, he's out the back. You wouldn't
go up and answer that for us, would you, Ivan?

IVAN: Yeah, no . . . *(Shoots his drink back and goes up the stairs)*

RICHARD: Ah, thanks, good man. *(Starts to sing tunelessly)* "Oh the
weather outside is frightening, it's dark and there's thunder
and lightning . . ." *(Suddenly hunches, holding his shoulders,
turning his face to the stairs)* Oh that draft is . . . Good fuck . . .

*(We hear voices from upstairs. Then we see Nicky's legs descend-
ing. It is completely dark outside by now.)*

NICKY *(Off)*: Oh yeah, yeah, yeah, yeah, yeah, no, yeah, all the
Christmas lights all up the . . . Aw no, no, no, no, no, no . . . We
won't stay long if he's . . . Come down, Mr. Lockhart!

(Nicky descends into the room followed by Ivan and Lockhart.)

RICHARD *(Rising)*: Nicky!

NICKY: Happy Christmas! Happy Christmas! Happy Christmas!

*(Nicky Giblin has a skinny, nervy appearance. He rarely seems
in bad humor. He is about Sharky's age or maybe younger. He
wears a tatty-looking anorak and threadbare gray slacks that are
slightly too short for him, revealing white sport socks in low-cut,
dark wine–colored slip-on shoes. Lockhart is a larger man in his
fifties perhaps. He is well-dressed in a camel-hair Crombie over-*

*coat, a silk scarf, a fine trilby hat and an expensive-looking suit.
He looks like a wealthy businessman and bon viveur. Both he and
Nicky glow warmly with festive indulgence.)*

RICHARD: And a happy Christmas to you, Nicky!

*(They embrace fondly. Nicky produces a gift-wrapped bottle of
whiskey from his anorak pocket.)*

NICKY: And I brought you just a little . . .

RICHARD *(Mildly remonstrating)*: Ah, Nicky . . .

NICKY *(Dismissive)*: Ah, go on, would you? Sure, where would you
be without the old Christmas, and I was just saying to . . .
Sorry, this is . . . Richard, this is Mr. Lockhart.

RICHARD: Mr. Lockhart! Pleased to meet you. Seasons greetings!

LOCKHART: And to you, too, Mr. Harkin. I hope you don't mind us
crashing in on you here now . . .

RICHARD: What are you talking about? Not at all! Not at all! Of
course not! Will you have a drop of . . . Nicky! We have Miller!
Ivan will you get a glass there for . . . I got Miller in especially
for you, Nicky. Ivan, it's in the . . . it's probably in the kitchen
there. Ask Sharky, will you?

NICKY: Is Sharky here?

RICHARD: Mr. Lockhart? Will you have a drop? Is this what I think
it is? Or a drop of stout or . . .

LOCKHART: I'll take a small Irish whiskey if you have it, Mr.
Harkin.

NICKY: And you do have it! Right there!

RICHARD: Ah, Nicky . . . And Mr. Lockhart, please, call me Richard
. . . Ivan, here will you . . . ? *(Holds the bottle out)*

IVAN: Ha?

RICHARD: Will you take this and . . . *(Thinks better of it)* or just
bring me a glass for Mr. Lockhart, and a bottle of Miller for
Nicky out of the fridge there, or it should be . . . just ask

Sharky. Please excuse me, Mr. Lockhart. Unfortunately my sight is . . . I fell into a dumpster at Halloween. I was attempting to retrieve a few rolls of wallpaper. I hit my noggin and I have no sight.

(Ivan goes to the kitchen.)

LOCKHART: God help you.

RICHARD: And this is my, this is my first Christmas here in the dark, so to speak . . . so it's eh . . .

LOCKHART: Yes.

NICKY: But the old mind burns brightly, Richard, ha?

RICHARD: Ah, well I don't know . . .

NICKY: No, no! To me, here now, sure you seem absolutely no different at all.

RICHARD: Ah, Nicky . . .

NICKY: No, it's true! So you got out for a Christmas drink?

RICHARD: Yes! We were down in Doyle's. Ivan was there and Big Bernard and Steady Eddie and the bouncy castle fella was singing hymns and, ah, it was brilliant . . .

(Ivan returns with a drink for Nicky, a glass for Lockhart and a glass for himself. The glasses are somewhat mixed and unsuitable but usable, e.g., perhaps he is using a little jug for himself.)

NICKY *(To Ivan)*: Is Sharky here?

IVAN: I think he's out in the . . .

RICHARD: Ah, he's doing a quick bit of . . . Don't mind him, he's off the drink—for Christmas!—and he has all our heads wrecked. So tell us, where were you? Here, Mr. Lockhart! *(Proffering bottle)*

(Nicky takes the bottle from Richard to pour a drink for Lockhart.)

NICKY: Where weren't we? Is the question! Good God—we've been . . . Well what happened was I'd a few bits to do with Eileen down in Killester, so she went off and I went into the Beachcomber—fucking nobody in it! *(To Lockhart)* What time was that at?

LOCKHART: About twelve?

NICKY: Twelve o'clock, nobody in there. I think, "Right I'll just have a quick pint and head on . . ." But then I see Mr. Lockhart is sitting up at the bar, who I know from up in the Marine . . . Mr. Lockhart, you'd do a lot of your drinking up in the Marine Hotel . . .

LOCKHART: I've been known to frequent the premises . . .

(They all laugh.)

NICKY: And we know each other from me calling up there to see my brother Eric . . . so we have a pint, but there was no atmosphere, so fuck it, we left—up to The Yacht.

LOCKHART: No, Harry Byrnes.

NICKY: Sorry, no, Harry Byrnes . . .

RICHARD: Oh very posh!

NICKY *(Pouring drinks for Lockhart, Richard and Ivan)*: Oh yeah, they had the fires lit and *then* we were in The Yacht . . . which was hopping.

RICHARD: Jaysus, yous were getting around!

NICKY: That was only the start of it! The Yacht, the Dollymount House . . .

LOCKHART: The Raheny Inn . . .

NICKY: The Raheny Inn, the Green Dolphin, the Station House, the Cedars, the Elphin—your man won't let me put my hand in my pocket—this is taxis everywhere now!

RICHARD: Very smart . . . God yous were . . .

NICKY: Then back all the way up to Edenmore, Eugene's, the Concorde . . . the bleeding Brookwood Inn! And then up here.

RICHARD: My God that's a right Christmas drink, Nicky!

NICKY: Yeah well Mr. Lockhart had to say happy Christmas to a few people ... *(Suddenly to Lockhart)* We never tracked them down!

LOCKHART: And I'm glad we didn't! Because we would never have made it up here! Anyway, as soon as a sing-along starts, I'm out of a place, that's just the way I am ... But we're here now, and that's it!

RICHARD: Well I'm glad you're here!

LOCKHART: Yes, and we'll say happy Christmas *(Raises his glass in a toast)* and we'll have a toast ...

NICKY *(Raising his drink)*: Yes.

(Ivan, who has just taken a big gulp of whiskey, spits the whiskey back into the glass for the toast.)

LOCKHART: To old friends and old times!

RICHARD: And new friends!

NICKY: Exactly! Cheers!

RICHARD: Happy Christmas!

NICKY: Happy Christmas!

(They all drink deeply.)

(Taking the bottle to give refills) So where's Sharky? God I haven't seen him in ages ...

RICHARD: Ivan, get Sharky there, will you? There's a good man.

IVAN: Yeah, I'll ...

(Ivan goes out through the kitchen.)

NICKY: How is he doing? All right?

RICHARD: Ah, Nicky, sure you know yourself. This is my brother, Mr. Lockhart. He claims he's here to look after me, but between ourselves, he's an awful useless fucking eejit, God help him. I don't know who's looking after who!

NICKY: Sure you'd be well able to look after yourself, Dick . . .

RICHARD: This is it. If they can get me one of those dogs that bring you your meals . . . or even someone just to do a tiny bit of shopping. Sure all I really need is the bit of company really.

NICKY: Well I knew you'd be up for a bit of companionship, and when I mentioned to Mr. Lockhart that there might be an old game of cards on the horizon, he was very eh . . .

LOCKHART: Well there's nothing like a game of cards at Christmas.

RICHARD: You're so right! And you're welcome, Mr. Lockhart. We're only amateurs now you understand.

NICKY: Go on out of that! You'll have to watch yourself, Mr. Lockhart, you'll be fleeced for Christmas!

RICHARD: Yeah, right!

LOCKHART: No fear! I'm not a big gambler myself necessarily. To be honest with you I just like the social . . . ness and the crack.

RICHARD: Well this is it! There's no big gamblers here, Mr. Lockhart. Why can't a game of cards be just for fun? You know what I mean?

(Sharky and Ivan enter from the kitchen. Sharky is wearing an apron and rubber gloves, and carrying a filthy cloth. Pause.)

NICKY: Ah, there you are, Sharky! Happy Christmas!

(Nicky goes to him to shake hands. Sharky removes a glove to shake his hand dutifully.)

SHARKY: Yeah, happy Christmas, Nicky.

NICKY: Eileen sends her regards. We hope you'll pop in over the . . .

SHARKY: Yeah, sure . . .

NICKY: This is Mr. Lockhart.

LOCKHART: Sharky. A pleasure.

SHARKY: How do you do.

(As they shake hands, Sharky wonders where he knows Lockhart from.)

NICKY: Mr. Lockhart said he'd pop in to help us make up the old numbers for a game of cards . . .

LOCKHART: I hope you don't mind, Sharky . . .

SHARKY *(Taking off his apron)*: No. I just didn't know we were playing cards.

NICKY: Ah, it's a tradition, Sharky! Ivan, you'll play . . .

IVAN: Well, yeah, I'll . . . But I've no . . . I've no money on me 'cause . . .

RICHARD: Don't worry about that, Ivan. Of course he'll play, we'll all play!

SHARKY *(To Richard)*: How will you read your cards?

RICHARD: Ivan and me'll play together! Ivan, you can read our cards and I'll bankroll us. How does that sound?

IVAN: Yeah, that's . . . that'd suit me . . .

RICHARD: And we'll split our takings fifty-fifty. Sure, I'm probably gonna have to bankroll Sharky anyway!

NICKY: Ivan'll be the eyes and Richard'll be the ears!

RICHARD: And the brains!

LOCKHART: Now you're sure I'm not barging in on your—

RICHARD: Not at all! Not at all! You're welcome. We'll take all of Nicky's money. Do you have any collateral, Nicky?

NICKY: Always. Feel that. *(Holds out his arm for Richard)*

RICHARD: Feel what?

NICKY: You feel that fabric?

(Richard feels the arm of Nicky's anorak.)

RICHARD: Oh nice!

NICKY: This is a Versace jacket.

RICHARD: Yes . . .

IVAN: Is it?

NICKY *(To Ivan)*: Feel that.

RICHARD: It's nice . . .

NICKY: You feel that? It's dog's skin.

IVAN: What?

NICKY *(Laughing)*: No, it's not dog's *skin*. It's called "dog's skin." It's German. Right, Mr. Lockhart?

LOCKHART: Yup.

RICHARD: It's nice, Nicky.

IVAN *(Incredulous)*: That's a Versace jacket?

NICKY *(Defensively)*: Yeah . . . Well . . . no, like it needs a wash for Christmas, only 'cause I wear it all the time, but it's eh . . . yeah, you know?

RICHARD: You might tell Sharky where he'd get a nice jacket like that, Nicky.

NICKY: Jacket like this? Two, three grand, Richard.

IVAN: What?!

NICKY: Oh big time! Oh here, Ivan, are you still driving that old orange Ford Fiesta?

IVAN: Yeah . . .

NICKY: 'Cause didn't we see, Mr. Lockhart? There was a load of old winos out there sitting on it, you don't want that.

IVAN: What? Is my car here?

NICKY: Yeah. *(To Lockhart)* Didn't I point it out to you? And I fucking said it . . .

LOCKHART: Yeah, it's parked up around the other side of the green, out there sort of half up on the path on the corner.

RICHARD *(Springing into action)*: Them fucking winos!! Come on, we can go out this way! Ivan, give me a hand. Show us where, Nicky.

(Richard goes toward the kitchen, taking hold of Ivan's arm.)

We won't be long, Mr. Lockhart. The winos are always scared of me. Drinking that old meths always has them nervy, you see. Sharky, you look after Mr. Lockhart. Come on! We'll have them gone out of it now, lickety-spit.

NICKY: We're not gonna be getting in a fight, are we?

RICHARD: No, no, they'll run off immediately. We'll be back in a minute. Come on, Ivan! Nicky, hit that light out there for yourselves.

NICKY: Yeah I got it.

(Nicky hits a switch in the kitchen as Ivan opens the back door and leads Richard out, followed by Nicky. Sharky and Lockhart are alone. Sharky shakes his head at Lockhart.)

LOCKHART: I know. Family, ha?

SHARKY: Yeah, don't talk to me. Are you okay for a drink there or . . .

LOCKHART: Yeah I'm grand. You not having a drink yourself?

SHARKY: Nah . . . I'm . . . trying to . . . not drink.

LOCKHART: If you can just beat Christmas, ha?

SHARKY *(A little laugh)*: Yeah . . .

LOCKHART: If I can just beat Christmas I can achieve anything!

SHARKY: Mmm.

LOCKHART: But it's so hard. 'Cause the old drink stops the brain cranking. Stops the mind going into the little cell.

(Sharky looks at Lockhart, wondering about him.)

I've seen you on your travels. You don't remember me, Sharky . . .

SHARKY *(Trying to place him)*: No I . . . I do . . .

LOCKHART: Yeah, I've seen you. On your wandering ways. I've seen you going down Wicklow Street, and halfway up Dame

Street, down Suffolk Street, Grafton Street, Dawson Street, round and round, back up, back down, am I right? *(Pause)* I've seen all those hopeless thoughts, buried there, in your stupid scrunched-up face.

SHARKY: What are you talking about?

LOCKHART: Oh come on, Sharky! You don't remember me?

SHARKY: No, I . . . I do. But where did we . . . ?

LOCKHART: We met in the Bridewell, Sharky.

(Short pause.)

Remember? We were locked up in a cell together. You'd had a bit of bother the night before? . . . You were waiting to go up before the judge . . . We played cards!

SHARKY: Yeah . . . no . . . I remember you but . . .

LOCKHART *(Brightly)*: So how have things been with you?

SHARKY: . . . Okay . . .

LOCKHART: Not great though . . .

(Pause.)

SHARKY: You've a good memory.

LOCKHART: Old as the hills, Sharky. You know I was sure I'd run into you today. *(Laughs)* But you're off the drink! Now that completely threw me, I have to say! Do you know how many pubs I was in?

SHARKY: Were you looking for me?

LOCKHART: Well, it's just that matter we discussed back then, in the Bridewell that night.

(Short pause.)

SHARKY: This has to be what? Twenty years ago!

LOCKHART: Twenty-five years ago. But considering what happened, I'm surprised you don't know why I'm here.

SHARKY: Yeah, well I don't.

LOCKHART *(Disappointed)*: Ah, Sharky . . . We had a deal. *(Short pause)* No?

SHARKY: Look I don't know what's going on here, or if Nicky's put you up to this, but I have to say I don't know what you're talking about.

LOCKHART: Are you serious?

SHARKY: Do I look like I'm telling a joke?

LOCKHART: No, hold on. Are you seriously trying to tell me . . . ? You're seriously standing there telling me that it's never struck you as odd? Down all these years that you just walked out of jail? After what you did? Ah, that's brilliant!

SHARKY: What do you mean "after what I did"?

LOCKHART: Oh, come on, now . . .

SHARKY: What? What did I . . . I can't even . . . What? I got into a fight with some wino in the back of a shebeen up in . . . Francis Street or . . . somewhere, was it? I can hardly even remember! So what?

LOCKHART: Well no, not quite. His name was Laurence Joyce. He was sixty-one. He was a vagrant. He said he was trying to get to Cardiff? . . . Said he had some family there? Said his wife was once the Cardiff Rose? . . . You beat him up in the back of O'Dowd's public house in the early hours of the twenty-fourth of December 1981. You killed him. *(Short pause)* I let you out. I set you free.

(Pause.)

SHARKY: No, here, wait a minute, if you're gonna . . .

LOCKHART: Come on, you remember that moment when the guards opened the door, in the morning? And told you to get your stuff and get lost?

SHARKY: . . . Yeah?

LOCKHART: I organized that. Because you won that hand of poker we were playing.

SHARKY: Wait a minute. That fella didn't die!

LOCKHART: Oh no. He did! Are you trying to tell me you don't see him in your nightmares?

(Pause. Sharky doesn't respond.)

God the poor old brain hasn't aged too well, has it, Sharky? Look at you. Twenty-five years on the lash like some old borderline wino yourself. What chance *haven't* you fucked up? Driving the van for those English fellas? The best years of your life with Eileen. What happened there? Tell me, are you still in the wars with Dublin Bus about the night you were drunk and you fell down the stairs? How much are you looking for, for that twinge in your back? You make me laugh, Sharky.

(Pause. Sharky is staring at Lockhart, dumbfounded.)

You even blew that chauffeur job down in Lahinch! *(Darkly)* You fancied your man's wife, didn't you?

SHARKY: Who are you again?

LOCKHART: Ah, Sharky . . . don't say you don't know who I am, don't make me say it.

SHARKY: I think maybe you should just leave.

LOCKHART: I want your soul, Sharky.

SHARKY: What?

LOCKHART: I want your soul.

SHARKY: What the hell are you talking about? Is this some kind of stupid fucking joke of Nicky's?

(Lockhart just looks at him. Sharky seems to feel queasy, then he enters the grip of some greater pain. It's so excruciating that he

starts to sink pathetically to his knees. He tries to get a grip on
something, but ends up on all fours, fighting the urge to pass out,
so great is the agony—both physically and deep within his mind.)

LOCKHART: I'm the son of the morning, Sharky. I'm the snake in
the garden. I've come here for your soul this Christmas, and
I've been looking for you all fucking day! We made a deal. We
played cards for your freedom and you promised me—you
promised me—the chance to play you again. So don't start
fucking me around now. *(Short pause)* Of course after you
skipped merrily off to some early house in the morning you
never even thought about it again, did you? You think I'm
messing about? You think you're better than me? Pig. Well
think again. Because we're gonna play for your soul and I'm
gonna win, and you're coming through the old hole in the
wall with me tonight, Sharky. Now get up.

(Sharky seems released from the pain. He struggles to get his
breath. He is silently crying as he staggers back to his feet.
Lockhart suddenly bursts toward him as though about to beat
him.)

No crying! Don't do a Maurice Macken on it! I'll fucking bat-
ter you! Do you hear me?

(Sharky flinches backward, blinking, a hand feebly raised.
Lockhart laughs.)

God love you, Sharky.

(There is a commotion outside as Nicky helps Richard back in
through the kitchen door, followed by Ivan.)

RICHARD *(On his way in)*: Them friggin' winos! They do my *head* in!

NICKY: You should've seen it! They ran for their lives!

RICHARD: Good Jaysus, would someone please give me a drink for the love of God?

NICKY (*Grabbing the whiskey bottle to give Richard a drink*): He blew them out of it! They flew off up the coast! You should have seen it!

(*Ivan comes in from the kitchen with a Miller for Nicky and a can of Harp for himself.*)

RICHARD: But was your man there? My little friend that I fucking hate with the navy anorak and the big black head of hair on him? He's the worst . . .

NICKY: Yeah, I think there was one like that. He fucking legged it! (*To Sharky and Lockhart*) The roars out of this fella . . .

RICHARD: Ah, you have to . . .

NICKY: And then Ivan!

RICHARD: I have Ivan well trained! You see they're so fucking nervy when they get that meths into them, you can destroy them with a good scream. I think they think it's the banshee, God help them.

NICKY: Did you see that one was going to the toilet down behind the car?

IVAN: I thought I saw one down in behind . . .

NICKY: That was a woman!

IVAN: Was it?!

RICHARD (*With disgust*): Oh, don't! . . .

NICKY (*Bursting out laughing*): It was all going down the back of her leg when she ran and fell over the bin!

RICHARD: Ah, stop, will you? They're awful . . .

LOCKHART (*To Ivan*): Is your car all right?

IVAN: Ah . . . it . . . it wasn't my car! I don't have my car with me. I forgot I walked up here in all the excitement.

RICHARD: Ah, well, all's well that end well! Are gonna play cards?

NICKY *(To Ivan)*: Can you see to play cards?

IVAN: I can see to about here. *(Holds his hand up about ten inches from his face)* After that, it's your guess is as good as mine!

RICHARD: Yeah, you can see the cards . . .

IVAN: I can read the cards . . .

RICHARD: Hey, Shark! Where's all the goodies you promised us that you were banging on about earlier? Get the smoked salmon and the mince pies out and all the Christmas goodies and the crisps and all . . . Are you hungry, Mr. Lockhart?

(Sharky is sitting to one side, contemplating his fate.)

LOCKHART *(Looking at Sharky)*: I wouldn't say no.

RICHARD: Well Sharky'll get the grub organized. Ivan pull out that table into the middle, the cards is on the windowsill.

(Nicky and Ivan begin to bustle about getting the table ready for cards.)

Another beer, Nicky?

NICKY: I have one. I'm good, Richard . . .

RICHARD: Mr. Lockhart? Another drop of Irish? Is it there? You can help yourself.

LOCKHART: I'm grand. Sharky's looking after me . . .

NICKY: I'm bursting for a slash, will I run in quickly?

RICHARD: No run up to the nice one, Nicky. Sharky! Is that upstairs loo in tip-top condition?

SHARKY: Yeah. You know where it is, Nicky.

NICKY: Yup, end of the landing.

(Nicky runs up the stairs.)

RICHARD: Ivan, there's stout there if you want a stout. I think I might have a stout actually.

IVAN: Good idea.

(Ivan goes into the kitchen.)

SHARKY: And don't mind Matt Talbot on the Kaliber there, he can look after himself. Is the table out?

LOCKHART: Here, Richard . . .

(Lockhart helps Richard to the table.)

RICHARD: Ah, thanks, Mr. Lockhart, you're a real gent. And don't mind Sharky's bad humor, he came out backwards, and his head has been arseways ever since. Here, give us the cards till I give them a shuffle.

(Lockhart hands the cards to Richard. Lockhart and Sharky stand looking at each other from opposite ends of the room.)

(Shuffling the cards) When Ivan comes back now he can cut them for me. *(Laughs)* I don't know whether these are up or down! I'm in total space here, Mr. Lockhart. Wheeee! And when Sharky has the grub for us and Nicky's back down we'll get going. God, I haven't played an old game of poker in so long! I'm really looking forward to it now. Ivan!

IVAN *(Off)*: Yeah?

RICHARD: Come on till we sort out this money!

IVAN *(Off)*: I'm coming, Dick! I'm just going to the jacks!

RICHARD: Come on, Nicky! Sit down, Mr. Lockhart, sit down. Sharky! Where's Sharky? Sharky, come on! Sharky!! . . . Let's play!!

(Blackout.)

A C T   T W O

M U S I C   I N   T H E   S U N

It is many hours later. The room is darker, seemingly lit only by a few lamps, candles and the glow from the stove. The wind is howling outside as a storm lashes the coast. The card game is in progress. Richard sits in the armchair which has been pulled nearer to the center of the room, closer to the table. He has a big box of chocolates nearby and munches one from time to time. To his left sits Ivan, who is at the edge of the table where he can play but also turn easily away from the others to consult strategy with Richard. Sharky sits to Ivan's left and Nicky sits to Sharky's left. Lockhart sits at the far end of the table. They are coming to the end of a round of heavy betting. The biggest piles of money are in front of Ivan and Lockhart. A lot of drink has been consumed; bottles, cans and empty plates are strewn around. Ivan's intoxication is constant, he coasts along, veering neither up into euphoria nor down into depression. It is his efficient life-state, removed, yet heavily present. Nicky, on the other hand, is an euphoric drunk. His genuine love for friends and comrades is freed. Richard, as we have seen, can lurch from sentimentality to vicious insults within seconds. But while all inhibitions may be gone, he remains alert, quick-witted and deeply interested in what goes on around him. Lockhart is a maudlin, philosophical drunk. Sharky has thus far managed to remain sober.

IVAN: Nicky . . .

NICKY: I'm thinking. I'm thinking.

RICHARD: I know. I can hear your brain crunching in your head from over here.

NICKY: Yeah, well don't be rushing me. What is it?

RICHARD: Mr. Lockhart raised it twenty. We're in. Sharky's bailed.

IVAN: You have to put in forty.

NICKY *(Takes a long sharp inhalation and thinks)*: . . . Yeah, well you're bluffing 'cause I saw Richard telling you . . .

RICHARD: Would you go on out of that!

NICKY: Mr. Lockhart is being cautious, he raised it twenty, but he's on a roll anyway, so he's battering us from a position of strength. *(To Ivan)* You have nothing.

IVAN *(Ironically)*: That's right.

NICKY: You have nothing! So stop with the . . . If you didn't have that pile in front of you, I'd have your guts for garters.

RICHARD: Why, what have we got?

NICKY: You've about two hundred and fifty fucking euros in front of you there, Dick.

RICHARD: Yo ho! Santy's come early!

IVAN *(Playing down their success)*: We're doing all right. We're doing nicely.

NICKY: And half of that is mine. *(With sudden confidence)* You have fuck all there, Ivan.

IVAN: Well why don't you make sure?

NICKY: Mr. Lockhart has two pair or something.

RICHARD: Well come on then!

NICKY: I am! *(Seeing and raising)* Here's your forty. And twenty now to show yous a statement of intent.

RICHARD: Oh ho . . .

NICKY: Now, that shook yous.

IVAN: Mr. Lockhart?

LOCKHART: I'll stick around. *(Sees Nicky's twenty)*

IVAN: And we'll have a look. *(Sees the twenty)*

(Pause. Nicky's courage seems to wane.)

NICKY *(To Ivan)*: What do you have?

IVAN *(To Nicky)*: What do you have?

RICHARD: What do we have?

IVAN *(To Nicky)*: What do you have?

NICKY *(To Lockhart)*: What do you have?

LOCKHART: Threes.

NICKY: Threes of what?

LOCKHART *(Shows his hand)*: Three nines.

NICKY: Three nines! You stuck it out with three nines?!

LOCKHART: I enjoy playing. Isn't it worth a go?

(Nicky bursts out laughing.)

RICHARD: What have you got, Nicky?

NICKY: Christmas present. Full house. *(Shows his hand)* Fives and kings.

IVAN *(Showing his hand)*: Kings and sevens.

NICKY: Bollocks!

(Richard whoops.)

Ah, that's fucking . . .

LOCKHART: Hard luck, Nicky . . .

NICKY *(To Lockhart)*: What were you doing driving the pot up the wazoo with three nines?! These lads are cleaning me out here!

RICHARD: Ah, Nicky . . .

NICKY: Look at me! I'm like Sharky here. I've about thirty-five euros to me name. This is to do me all through January . . .

(Nicky gets up and walks over to the stove, restlessly.)

IVAN *(Counting his winnings)*: Well Sharky had the right idea. He bailed. He knew.

RICHARD: He has no money!

IVAN: Do you want a stout, Rich?

RICHARD: Sure! Hey! You know what I have in there of course, beside the boiler? There's a drop of Brigid Blake's famous Antrim poteen in there.

IVAN: Oh ho!

RICHARD: Do you ever take a drop, Mr. Lockhart?

(Ivan heads toward the kitchen.)

LOCKHART: I will! Why not? Sure I might as well be shit-faced as the way I am!

IVAN *(On his way into the kitchen)*: Yo ho!

RICHARD: Good man!

NICKY: Yeah, well leave me out of it . . . Grab us a Miller there, Ivan, would you?

IVAN *(Off)*: Yeah!

NICKY: Ah, well . . . it's only a game. It's only money, that right, Rich?

RICHARD: Yeah . . . Your money!

(Nicky sighs heavily, looking to Lockhart in a silent appeal for understanding.)

NICKY: So, Sharky! You're back! *(Drunkenly placing a hand on Sharky's shoulder)* We've missed you! D'you know that? *(Turns to Lockhart, pointing at Sharky meaninglessly, then turns back to Sharky)*

RICHARD *(Insincerely)*: Yeah . . . we've all missed you . . .

NICKY: So tell us! Where's this you were working?

SHARKY: Ah, down in Lahinch, County Clare.

NICKY: On the trawlers . . . ?

SHARKY: No.

NICKY *(Surprised)*: No?

SHARKY: No I was eh . . . *(Glancing at Lockhart who is smiling at him broadly)* I was doing a bit of driving for a fella down there.

NICKY: Lahinch? Was I reading somewhere or where was it? That Lahinch is the gay-pickup capital of Ireland?

SHARKY: What?

NICKY: So I believe . . .

(Ivan returns with a whiskey bottle full of poteen.)

SHARKY: No . . .

RICHARD: Ah, Nicky, Lahinch is only a small town, how could it possibly be the gay-pickup capital of Ireland?

NICKY: Well *I* don't know!

RICHARD: The gay-pickup capital of Ireland is Cork City!

NICKY: Is it?

RICHARD: It very probably is.

IVAN *(To Lockhart)*: Richard hates the Cork people . . .

RICHARD: Well that's not my fault! They need to look to themselves, not me! I wash me hands of it! Are you pouring us a drop of that moon juice, Ivan?

IVAN: Will I open it?

RICHARD: Yes.

NICKY: Did you get me a Miller?

IVAN: Did you ask me for one?

NICKY: Yes!

IVAN: Oh sorry I didn't hear you.

(Ivan goes back into the kitchen.)

NICKY: Thanks, Ivan. I wouldn't touch that brain blower now if you paid me . . . Look out, Mr. Lockhart, you'll be bollixed.

RICHARD: No he won't! It'll help him play!

NICKY: It will in my arse! Steady Eddie was hallucinating that traffic wardens were coming to arrest him in the snooker club in Harmonstown one morning after he'd been skulling that shite the night before!

RICHARD: Ah, he's a child! Don't mind him, Mr. Lockhart.

LOCKHART: No, I'll have a drop.

RICHARD: Good man.

NICKY: Well I don't mind if you all start losing!

(Ivan returns, making his way to the table to pour some drinks.)

Thanks, Ivan. Good to see you, Shark. Of course you know I'm in a totally new line now myself?

SHARKY: What, you're not doing the babysitting?

NICKY: No, I'm out of the babysitting. I'm out of that this long weather now. Too many trust issues, essentially. Not on my part. No, I'm gone into the cheese-mongering business.

SHARKY: Cheese-mongering?

(Ivan pours some poteen for Richard and Lockhart.)

NICKY: Yeah, I've me own counter down the back of Thrifties.

SHARKY: Have you?

NICKY: Yup. I'm only started it, but it could be a whole new empire.

SHARKY: Do you not have to study for years to do something like that?

NICKY *(Incredulous)*: What?!

SHARKY: I thought you had to study to do cheese and wines and all . . . to do it properly . . .

NICKY: No you don't! Who told you that?

SHARKY: I don't know. No, I just thought . . .

NICKY: No you don't! *(Laughs)* Whoever told you that now is . . . Ah, poor Sharky! Aw God . . . Ah, d'you know who was asking for you yesterday? When your name came up in conversation? Young Carla, Eileen's daughter.

SHARKY: Oh yeah?

NICKY: Yeah, big shock to hear her ask about anything . . .

SHARKY: How is she doing?

NICKY *(Not too positively)*: Ah, she's . . . You always see her hanging round down the shops, down around the shopping center. *(To Lockhart)* I do do a lot of my drinking in Madigan's in the shopping center, Mr. Lockhart. She's always walking that bloody dog! What is it?

SHARKY: It's a terrier.

RICHARD: Is this the little young one used come in here with you, Sharky?

SHARKY: Yeah.

RICHARD: How old is she, now?

NICKY: Oh she's fifteen or sixteen now, Rich.

RICHARD: Is she?

NICKY: Oh yeah, she's packed in the school! She's gonna be a hairdresser. She says, anyway.

RICHARD: Do you remember her, Sharky? She was always chatting away in here, she was hilarious . . .

SHARKY: Mmm.

NICKY: Well not anymore. She's as moody . . . she's a real little . . . anyway, she was asking for you, Shark.

SHARKY: How's the car?

NICKY: What car?

SHARKY: The Peugeot.

NICKY: Eileen's car?

SHARKY: Well, it's my old car actually.

NICKY: Oh is it?

SHARKY: Yeah.

NICKY: Did you get a new one?

(Pause.)

RICHARD: No, he didn't! Sure where would Sharky get a new car? *(Raising his glass of poteen)* Your health, Mr. Lockhart!

NICKY: Say good-bye to it!

LOCKHART: No, this is smooth!

NICKY: Yeah, a smooth operator . . .

LOCKHART: You know this is the only time of the year I really enjoy? A game of cards on Christmas Eve, sure where would you get it?

RICHARD: Absolutely!

IVAN: You play a lot of cards, Mr. Lockhart?

LOCKHART: Well . . . I do at Christmas! Boys, I've played cards in public houses, shebeens, hotel barrooms, suburban boozers—anywhere! Three, four in the morning, nobody there, only a few auld lads in their shirtsleeves, tidying up while they watch some poor fucking eejit play it all away . . . Houses! Little houses . . . on Christmas Eve . . . in the middle of nowhere I've played. Out on the western seaboard, but mostly in the east. Ah, I've played everywhere! You name it! In police stations . . . Sharky, out the back of beyond. Up in amazing Georgian rooms with wonderful evocative gilt mirrors and beautiful windows towering out onto incredible trees—in the middle of Dublin, or London, in the city, yup. A school or two I've played in. In my time. Always late. It's always so late . . . Time deepens and slows down somehow in a card game. It could be any moment. It's always the same moment . . . Where do I know you from, Ivan?

IVAN: Ha?

LOCKHART: Have we played cards?

SHARKY: No, I don't think you have . . .

IVAN: Yeah, we might of . . .

LOCKHART: You're the fella won the boat that time in a card game, Nicky was telling me . . .

NICKY: Yeah.

IVAN *(Modestly)*: Well . . .

RICHARD: No, he did, that's right.

IVAN *(To Richard)*: Do you remember that, Dick?

RICHARD: I sure do!

NICKY: Forty grand's worth of boat, Mr. Lockhart!

IVAN: Yeah but I sold it for twelve. I didn't want it! What would I want with a fucking boat?

NICKY: It only would've cost him money anyway . . .

IVAN: I sold it for twelve grand up in the Cock Tavern in Howth— do you remember, Richard? Best Christmas ever!

RICHARD: Ah, brilliant. It was brilliant!

NICKY: You could never top that!

IVAN: I lost it all in three weeks, Mr. Lockhart. Betting in the book- ies in Baldoyle and practically living in Doyle's Lounge. I was eating so much fish and chips and battered sausages at all weird hours and I saw fuck-all daylight . . .

NICKY: This is all true!

IVAN: . . . that I ended up getting the runs so bad and I was so dehydrated the doctor wouldn't let me out of the house for four whole days!

(Richard, Nicky and Ivan are laughing.)

It was unbelievable! It was an absolutely unbelievable Christ- mas. Do you remember all the stars we saw that Stephen's Night, Nicky?

NICKY *(Too beautiful to describe)*: Aw!

IVAN: Yeah, but you panic though when it starts to run right down. Oh Jaysus, if Karen had've known I'd had all that . . . Oh! *(Shudders)* Had to get rid of it.

LOCKHART: Yeah, and you won it just in a card game in a house?

IVAN: Yeah, won it off a total nutcase that killed himself not long after. He drownded after driving his car off the end of the pier in Howth.

NICKY: The Briquette King.

IVAN: He had a business delivering peat briquettes . . .

RICHARD: He was a nasty piece of work, Mr. Lockhart . . .

NICKY: Aw, he was a real prick!

LOCKHART: Yeah? God, that's a great story. But you know what I was wondering, after Nicky told me about it, I wanted to ask you . . . Look at Sharky looking at me suspiciously there . . . no I was just wondering, with the stakes so high—a forty-grand boat, like—I was wondering what you had in the pot that he was betting his boat against you?

IVAN: Ha?

LOCKHART: No, just what did you have in the pot to put up against his boat? I'm assuming there couldn't have been forty grand in the pot. In a card game like the way we're playing now . . . What did you have, that he wanted? . . .

(Ivan looks at Nicky. Pause.)

SHARKY: Here look, are we gonna play here?

LOCKHART: You don't have to tell me . . .

RICHARD: It was stupid! Your man was out of it!

NICKY: He was a lunatic! He was acting the bollocks. Ivan took him down fair and square.

LOCKHART: It was something to do with that hotel down in Wicklow, was it?

(Long pause.)

SHARKY *(To Lockhart)*: What are you doing?

LOCKHART: You told me something about that, Nicky, didn't you? About Ivan and what was it? The Ardlawn Hotel?

NICKY *(Guiltily)*: No . . .

RICHARD *(Disappointed)*: Nicky . . .

NICKY: I didn't . . .

SHARKY: Let's just play, will we? That's got nothing to do with anything.

LOCKHART: What was the name of those two families?

IVAN *(In a dark place)*: The Murdochs and the Kavanaghs.

LOCKHART: That's right . . .

RICHARD: That was all in the news. Ivan was completely exonerated . . .

NICKY: It was inconclusive . . .

SHARKY: Yeah. Hey, look . . . Can we just get on with the . . .

(Sharky takes a sharp intake of breath and puts his hand to his head in sudden immense pain.)

NICKY: Are you all right, Shark?

SHARKY *(Blinking)*: Yeah, no, I'm . . .

RICHARD: Leave him alone. He just needs a drink. That whole thing was an open-and-shut case, Mr. Lockhart . . .

LOCKHART: What happened? There was a fire? . . .

IVAN: Yeah, well . . . It was twenty-odd years ago. It was more . . .

NICKY: Ancient history . . .

IVAN: I was working in the Ardlawn. I was doing a bit of portering and bit of night-portering . . .

RICHARD: Ivan was completely exonerated.

NICKY: There was no blame.

IVAN: No, they had to investigate it. I had . . . you see I had burned my hand on the ring of a cooker when I was . . . I was heating some beans . . . it was very late and . . . *(Pause)* This was all in the papers!

LOCKHART: Yeah . . . but it can really hang over a man, something like that . . .

IVAN: Well, yeah, the . . . this fella with the boat, the briquette king. He wanted to play for . . .

NICKY: He was a wanker.

IVAN: The bet was that he could . . . if he won, he wanted to ask me . . . what happened? I don't know . . .

LOCKHART: To give him the truth.

(Pause.)

IVAN: Yeah . . .

NICKY: It was a ridiculous fucking bet . . . He was a sick fucking eejit and that's all that was going on. And he got his come-uppance!

RICHARD: He's gone and good luck to him. He was a bully.

LOCKHART: High stakes, Ivan . . .

IVAN: Yeah . . . well I'd a strong hand.

LOCKHART: Yeah. I knew there had to be something . . . You don't mind talking about it . . .

(Pause.)

NICKY: I hate that fucking poteen! The fucking smell of it, even!

RICHARD: Ah, stop giving out! Are we gonna play cards? There's too much auld lang syne going on around here and not enough cards!

NICKY: Yeah, well let's play, come on!

RICHARD: Whose deal is it? Sharky! You deal!

LOCKHART: Yes! We haven't hardly had a burst out of Sharky tonight at all!

RICHARD: Ah, Sharky could never play cards!

NICKY *(Gathering up the cards to give to Sharky)*: I've seen Sharky win.

LOCKHART: Maybe he's preoccupied.

RICHARD: Ah, he's always preoccupied . . .

NICKY: Come on. Two euros to play. Maybe this is Sharky's hand.

RICHARD: Give us a drop of that holy water, Ivan, till we bless ourselves.

NICKY: Little threes is all I need.

(Sharky shuffles the cards to deal. Everyone puts in two euros. Ivan puts in four, to cover himself and Richard, then he gets up to pour a drink for Richard.)

IVAN: Richard . . .

RICHARD *(To Ivan)*: Good man. *(Raising his glass)* Mr. Lockhart?

LOCKHART: I will! Thank you, Ivan.

RICHARD: Hey, Mr. Lockhart . . .

(Lockhart looks at Richard who points to his head and makes a whistling sound to indicate the effect of the poteen.)

LOCKHART: I know! I'm fucking slipping in and out of time zones here. I thought it was last Christmas there for a minute!

RICHARD: Yes! That's right!

(Ivan goes to pour a drink for Lockhart.)

NICKY: Yeah, well leave me out of it. I want to stay here in this Christmas and beat the shite out of yous now with this hand. I can feel it in me waters. Little threes there now, Sharky. Get us a Miller there, Ivan, will you?

(Ivan goes to get a beer for Nicky.)

IVAN: Do you want another Seven-Up, Shark?

SHARKY: Nah, I'm all right . . .

RICHARD: Oh, threes is a beaut . . .

NICKY: That's my killer hand, is three threes.

RICHARD: Yeah, I love three tens. Three tens is my . . .

LOCKHART: Ah, a ten is like a shining tower. It's like the twentieth century. It's solid. It towers, yeah?

RICHARD: Absolutely.

NICKY: Well I also like to see an eight. Give me a pair of eights for starters and I'm—

RICHARD (*Dismissively*): Ah, eight! Eight is sneaky . . . Look at it! What is it? Eight! It's not a ten, it's almost as bad as a nine . . .

LOCKHART: Well nine can have a certain symmetry to it.

NICKY: Oh, three threes is a lovely little hand. It's like a little grenade.

RICHARD: And seven . . .

LOCKHART: Oh, seven is deep.

(*Ivan returns with beers for Nicky and himself.*)

NICKY (*To Ivan*): We're talking about numbers.

IVAN (*Unconvinced*): Ah, seven is only my hole. Give me a four.

SHARKY: Yeah . . .

IVAN: Four is where you build your house.

(*They all pick up their cards and peruse them.*)

LOCKHART (*To Ivan*): Do you not have two fours in front of you there?

IVAN: That's a secret, Mr. Lockhart.

NICKY: Ah, nice try! Mr. Lockhart is no slouch!

RICHARD: Well neither is Ivan! How are we doing? Who's it to?

SHARKY: Ivan?

IVAN: Ah, check . . .

SHARKY: Nicky?

NICKY: Eh . . . I'll check for a minute.

SHARKY: Mr. Lockhart . . .

LOCKHART: Ah, sure we'll make it interesting anyway. *(Putting in coins)* Three euros.

RICHARD: Will we stick around for three euros, Ivan?

IVAN: We'll see what happens. *(Puts in coins)*

SHARKY: Nicky?

NICKY: Ah, we'll hang around. *(Sees the bet)*

SHARKY: And I'll have a look. *(Sees it and picks up the deck to deal)* Ivan?

IVAN: Eh . . . Three please, Sharky.

(Sharky deals him three cards.)

LOCKHART: Little pair of fours there, Ivan?

RICHARD: Don't tell him nothing!

IVAN: I'm not . . .

SHARKY: Nicky.

NICKY: Eh . . . two . . .

(Sharky deals him two cards. Nicky suddenly throws down one more card.)

No, three . . .

SHARKY: You sure?

NICKY: Yeah, three, thanks.

(Sharky deals another card to Nicky.)

SHARKY: Mr. Lockhart?

LOCKHART: Just one, please, Sharky.

(Reactions to this around the table. Sharky deals him a card.)

RICHARD: Just the one, Mr. Lockhart?

LOCKHART: Just the one . . .

NICKY: Ah, he's on a kamikaze. What is it? A run? Flush? Did you get it?

LOCKHART: Maybe it's four of a kind.

RICHARD: Maybe it's total bollocks.

LOCKHART: Maybe . . .

SHARKY: And I'll take three. To you, Mr. Lockhart.

LOCKHART: Ah, we'll keep the dream alive. Sure five euros. *(Puts in money)*

RICHARD: Oh look out . . .

SHARKY: Ivan?

IVAN: Ehm . . . We'll hang on. *(Sees the bet)*

RICHARD: We'll hang on for a minute . . .

SHARKY: Nicky?

NICKY: Ah, we'll go along for the ride. *(Sees it) And* we'll make it interesting. Ten euros.

(Reactions around the table.)

RICHARD: Oh now!

SHARKY: Mr. Lockhart?

LOCKHART: I'll see you . . . with ten.

RICHARD: Oh now, here! What are we doing? Ivan!

NICKY *(To Lockhart)*: You fucker . . .

(Ivan leans over to whisper to Richard who listens intently.)

RICHARD: Ah, fold, for fuck's sake! Would you? Jaysus . . .

IVAN *(Throws his hand in)*: We're gone.

SHARKY: Nicky?

NICKY *(Considers Lockhart)*: I'll see you. *(Puts in ten)*

RICHARD: You're a fucking eejit . . .

NICKY: Hold your horses. Stranger things have happened at sea . . .

RICHARD *(Dismissive)*: Yeah, right . . .

LOCKHART: Sharky?

RICHARD: Don't be a hero now, Sharky . . .

SHARKY *(Considers his hand)*: So what is it?

NICKY: It's twenty-five for you to play, Shark. And I'd advise you to tread warily against what I have here now . . .

RICHARD: Easy now, Sharky. I'm not keeping you in pocket money for the whole of next month now, right?

SHARKY: Twenty-five. *(Sees it and reaches into his pocket, taking some money out)* With twenty-five.

RICHARD: What!?

IVAN: Ah, let him play, Rich.

LOCKHART: Brave man . . .

NICKY: To you, Mr. Lockhart . . .

LOCKHART: I'm in. *(Sees the bet)*

(Nicky looks at his cards.)

IVAN: Nicky . . .

NICKY: I'm thinking. I'm thinking. I'm thinking. I'm thinking.

RICHARD: I *thought* there was a funny smell . . .

NICKY: Ha ha . . . *(To Lockhart, putting money in)* Come on! What do you have?

(Pause.)

LOCKHART *(Shows his hand)*: I've nothing.

NICKY: You bastard! What were you doing?!

LOCKHART: I wanted to move it on, get you in, keep things interesting. We're playing a game!

NICKY: You fucking eejit. That's that poteen. I told you . . .

IVAN: It could be yours, Nicky . . .

RICHARD: It better not be!

IVAN: Go on, Nicky! What do you have?

(Pause.)

NICKY: Ah, I've even less nothing. I've a hand of feet. Half a run. I knew he *(Referring to Lockhart)* had nothing. I thought it'd be too pricey for Sharky. What have you got, Shark, two pair or some fucking thing . . .

SHARKY: Not even. One pair.

NICKY: One pair?! *(Grabs Sharky's cards)* Two fucking fours?!

IVAN: It still beats you.

LOCKHART: Nicely played, Sharky . . .

(Nicky throws the cards on the table and stands up.)

NICKY: A hundred euros with two fours! *(Paces around, going toward the stove)*

SHARKY: Your deal, Nicky . . .

(Nicky kicks a wall.)

NICKY: Bollocks!

RICHARD: Oy! Oy! Nicky, don't destroy the place.

NICKY: No, no. I'm sorry, Richard.

IVAN: Nice one, Sharky . . .

NICKY *(Taking money from his wallet)*: What were we all doing? *(To Lockhart)* You had nothing!? I had fuck-all! And Sharky wins a hundred euro with two fucking fours!

LOCKHART: Luck of the draw.

NICKY: What were you doing raising all the time?

LOCKHART: You were raising as well.

NICKY: Ah, I was only having a go! Here, give us some change there, Ivan.

LOCKHART: It's only money . . .

(Nicky goes to Ivan's pile to get some smaller denominations, throwing two twenty-euro notes down.)

RICHARD: Ah, hard luck, Nicky, sure it's only a bit of fun . . .

NICKY: I won't be having much more fun at this rate . . .

RICHARD: You could never bluff, Nicky. That's just something you can't . . .

IVAN *(Pointing at Sharky)*: You see him? King of the bluffers.

RICHARD: Who? Sharky?

IVAN: Yeah.

RICHARD: Yeah, well, that's only because he has a recklessness in his heart, which is the undoing and ruination of his whole life.

IVAN: Not tonight.

RICHARD: Yeah? Just wait. Ah, cheer up, Nicky.

NICKY: Yeah, well give me a few minutes! . . . That's a harsh lesson there now.

LOCKHART: Only kind . . .

IVAN: Well, Sharky's around for another few hands in anyway . . .

RICHARD: He should quit while he's ahead.

LOCKHART: Don't worry, Nicky. I'm gonna take Sharky down.

NICKY: Can I bet on it?

LOCKHART: Nothing surer.

RICHARD: Ah, would you come on and deal the cards and stop moaning. You'll probably trounce us all this time out.

NICKY *(Taking the cards to give them a shuffle)*: I hope so!

RICHARD *(Handing the box of sweets to Ivan)*: Here, Ivan, pass them around.

IVAN: Oh, nice one!

(A mobile phone starts ringing somewhere.)

RICHARD: What's that music?

NICKY: Oh bollocks! That's my phone!

RICHARD: Oh, here's trouble . . .

IVAN: I'm not here . . .

(Nicky goes to his jacket and rummages for his phone.)

NICKY: It's Eileen!

IVAN: Well, whoever it is, I'm not here.

(They all wait as Nicky stands looking at his phone.)

NICKY: I'm gonna have to answer this, Dick.

RICHARD: Well, would you answer the Jaysus thing and stop driving us all around the fucking twist!

(Nicky answers it.)

NICKY *(Very innocently)*: Hello?

(The others are listening.)

Hi, hon. What? No! No, I'm just visiting poor Richard to see if he . . . No. No, Sharky's here. Yeah. No, he's here. He's not even drinking. And I'm only . . . I'm just having a very quick bottle of Miller. No, I swear to God, he isn't! What? Yeah. No, I'll be back. No, don't try lifting it down yourself . . . No, no, I'll do it! *(Drifts upstage toward the staircase and upstairs out of earshot of the others)* No, I'll be there! What's wrong with you? It's Christmas! What? Hold on, just let me . . . *(He is gone)*

RICHARD: Trouble in Paradise.

IVAN: Don't talk to me about trouble in Paradise! Here, will I put on some music?

RICHARD: Oh yes! Good idea! Good idea!

(Ivan wanders over to the stereo.)

LOCKHART: Hey, hold on, are we not gonna . . . ? *("play")*

RICHARD: Music to soothe the soul. What kind of music do you like, Mr. Lockhart?

LOCKHART: I don't really like music.

(Ivan puts on some festive music, softly.)

RICHARD: How can you not like music? *Any* music?

LOCKHART: I don't like any music.

RICHARD: Do you hear that, Ivan? Mr. Lockhart doesn't like *any* music!

IVAN: Sure that's impossible.

RICHARD: That's what I would've thought.

LOCKHART: No, you see . . . I can't hear it.

IVAN: What, are you tone-deaf?

LOCKHART: No, no, I just don't like the sound. You see, to me it's just an ugly noise.

RICHARD: Dear God! That's a terrible affliction. Sure you can hardly escape music!

IVAN: What? Like, do you want me to turn it off?

LOCKHART: If you don't mind.

(Ivan stands there, hoping Lockhart will relent.)

That would be most agreeable.

(Ivan goes and turns off the music. Pause.)

RICHARD: Lordy, lordy, lordy, lordy, lordy, lordy, lordy, lordy, lordy, would you listen to that wind? God, I had an awful dream the other night. I dreamt I could see. I dreamt that I woke up and I could see, and that being blind had been a dream. And I dreamt the sun was shining in through the window there, and there, just sitting on the windowsill was a bluebottle, or a horsefly, looking at me. You ever notice about those things? The whole head is nearly their eyes. Two big black footballs on the whole two sides of their head. And I was just staring at him and he was just staring at me—as much as you can tell if he's "looking" at you at all . . . "What does he think of

me?" I was wondering, as we were kind of . . . communing
with each other there. And there was such . . . comfort, in his
blank unseeing regard for me, Mr. Lockhart. You just know
that God is in a fly, don't you? The very existence and the
amazing design in something so small and intricate as a bluebottle—it's God's revelation really, isn't it? Don't you think
that?

LOCKHART: Well . . . except that they seem to like the taste of shit
so much, don't they?

RICHARD: Ah, that only adds to their intrigue . . .

LOCKHART: If you say so.

RICHARD: Well I do! I do say so! And . . . But then I had the terrible misfortune to wake up and . . . and I realized I couldn't see.
And I kind of . . . I kind of panicked. I didn't know if it was
night, or day, or what the hell it was, or where I was. And
I didn't want to call out to Sharky, because in case I woke him,
his moods do be bad enough! And I . . . or turn on the radio
in case I woke him, but I got my bearings. I was down here
and I thought, "If I can get a drop of whiskey, the old panic
may subside." But then of course, I fell in the fucking kitchen
door and I made such a clatter that Sharky woke up anyway!
Didn't you?

SHARKY: Yeah, well, I wasn't asleep. But Jaysus . . . I thought someone was breaking in. Bottles smashing all over the floor . . .

RICHARD: Yeah! What was it? It was . . .

SHARKY: It was five o'clock in the bleeding morning.

RICHARD: Yeah, well we were up then, weren't we?

SHARKY: Yeah.

RICHARD: Then your man (*Referring to Sharky*) wants to give me
a bath! (*Pronounced "bat"*)

LOCKHART: A what?

(*Ivan goes around with the poteen topping up their drinks.*)

RICHARD: A bat! He wants to wash me! And bathe me, the fucking . . . (*"eejit"*)

LOCKHART: Well, he's trying to be what's known as "a good
person."

RICHARD: Well he should give up! (*Laughs*) Hey, Sharky, what
about that . . . (*Touches his groin*)

SHARKY (*Remembering with disgust*): Oh! . . .

RICHARD: Ivan, there was a . . . what would you call it, Sharky?

SHARKY: I don't want to talk about it.

RICHARD: It was like a lump of . . . up here at the top of me leg
where the crease meets the . . .

SHARKY: Aw, would you fucking stop, Richard?

RICHARD: It was hard, now. And deeply . . . embedded in the . . .

SHARKY: Ah, Richard!

RICHARD: Like either congealed . . . or . . . the smell when Sharky
started rubbing it!

(*Nicky descends.*)

SHARKY: Richard!

RICHARD: And the fucking pain of it . . . Sharky going at it with
the nailbrush! And the smell!

NICKY: What's this?

RICHARD: Nicky, I had this . . .

SHARKY: No, come on, that's it now. . . . Jesus Christ . . .

RICHARD (*Angrily*): Ah, I'm only trying tell a fucking story here,
Jim, what's fucking wrong with you, for Jaysus' sake?! (*Short
pause. To Nicky*) I'll tell you later . . .

(*Short pause.*)

NICKY: Well, I've got about an hour's parole, so let's get on with
the cards, because if I want to have any chance of . . .

(There is a sudden loud bang at the back door out through the kitchen. They all fall silent, listening.)

What the fuck is that?

RICHARD *(Getting up)*: That's them fucking winos! Where's me stick? Ivan!

SHARKY: Ah, Rich, come on ... don't be ...

(Nicky goes into the kitchen, peering out the back door into the gloom.)

RICHARD: Don't fucking start now, Sharky! You don't know what I have to live with! I'm sorry, Mr. Lockhart, we have an awful problem with these winos out in the lane. Come on, Ivan!

IVAN: They're probably gone, they just ...

NICKY: I think they must have thrown something or ...

IVAN: Put the light on out there, Nicky.

(Richard has a hold of Ivan.)

RICHARD: Come on, Ivan. Come on, Nicky. Open that back door for me.

NICKY: Hey, hold on, is there something I can ...?

RICHARD: There's an old golf club in there beside the jacks door, Nicky.

IVAN: Put the light on out there, Nicky, will you?

(Nicky finds the golf club and hits a light in the backyard.)

NICKY: Hold on now, Rich, now I don't see anyone.

RICHARD: Come on, we'll get them in the lane.

SHARKY: Richard, put your coat on, will you?

RICHARD: Ah, we're all right, we'll just chase them off.

IVAN: They'll be gone I'd say anyway.

(Nicky opens the back door and goes out into the wind. Richard and Ivan follow. Richard does a native Indian whooping sound by vibrating his open palm in front of his mouth while letting out a high-pitched shout.)

RICHARD *(Making his way out)*: Keep a hold of me now, Ivan!
NICKY *(Off)*: Hey, mind with that stick, will ya?
RICHARD: Sorry, Nicky!

(The back door shuts. Sharky and Lockhart are alone. Pause.)

LOCKHART: Well, Sharky. You ready to come with me?
SHARKY: You haven't beaten me yet.
LOCKHART *(Getting up to pour himself more poteen)*: No, not yet, I'm enjoying myself too much! I'll hammer you now in this next hand. And then I'll take you right through the old hole in the wall.

(Lockhart pours himself a drink. He sways, then falls over.)

Woops.
SHARKY: Mind you don't fall.
LOCKHART: Well to tell you the truth, I never drink this much.
SHARKY: Yeah, well welcome to our house.

(Lockhart stands with his drink. He raises his free hand to look at it in the light.)

LOCKHART: I hate these stupid insect bodies you have. *(Switches his drink from one hand to another)* This fucker is left-handed! *(Looking down at his legs)* I mean, what is it? What are human beings? Two balloons—that's your lungs—and an annoying little whistle at the top where the air comes out—that's your voice . . . *(Pause. Shouting)* I mean what have you got that

I haven't?! Hey, Romeo. *(Short pause)* I'm talking to you, Love's Young Dream! What have you got? Ha? You all age and wither before me like dead flowers in a bright window! You're nothing! Me? I live in the stars above St. Anne's Park! Thousands of Christmas Eves I've seen! I'm so old . . . and thousands more I'll see—maybe millions! I'm the very power that keeps us apart! Isn't that worth saving? *(Beat)* Evidently not. No, He loves you. He loves all you insects . . . *(Lost and distant)* Figure that one out.

(Pause.)

SHARKY: What'll happen to me? If I lose.
LOCKHART: When you lose.
SHARKY: If I lose.
LOCKHART: You're going to hell.

(Short pause.)

SHARKY: What is it?
LOCKHART: What's hell? *(Gives a little laugh)* Hell is . . . *(Stares gloomily)* Well, you know, Sharky, when you're walking round and round the city and the streetlights have all come on and it's cold. Or you're standing outside a shop where you were hanging around reading the magazines, pretending to buy one 'cause you've no money and nowhere to go and your feet are like blocks of ice in those stupid little slip-on shoes you bought for chauffeuring. And you see all the people who seem to live in another world all snuggled up together in the warmth of a tavern or a cozy little house, and you just walk and walk and walk and you're on your own and nobody knows who you are. And you don't know anyone and you're trying not to hassle people or beg, because you're trying not to drink, and you're hoping you *won't* meet anyone you know

because of the blistering shame that rises up in your face and you have to turn away because you know you can't even deal with the thought that someone might love you, because of all the pain you always cause. Well that's a fraction of the self-loathing you feel in hell, except it's worse. Because there truly is no one to love you. Not even Him. *(Points to the sky)* He lets you go. Even He's sick of you. You're locked in a space that's smaller than a coffin. Which is lying a thousand miles down just under the bed of a vast, icy, pitch black sea. You're buried alive in there. And it's so cold that you can't even feel your angry tears freezing in your eyelashes and your very bones ache with deep perpetual agony and you think, "I must be going to die . . ." But you never die. You never even sleep because every few minutes you're gripped by a claustrophobic panic and you get so frightened you squirm uselessly against the stone walls and the heavy lid, and your heart beats so fast against your ribs you think, "I *must* be going to die . . ." But of course . . . you never will. Because of what you did. *(Pause. Sharky stares into his bleak eternal fate)* That's where I am too, Sharky. I know you see me here in this man's clothes, but that's where I really am . . . *(Short pause)* Oh you'd have loved heaven, Sharky. It's *unbelievable!* Everyone feels peaceful! *(Laughs)* Everyone feels at such peace! Because your mind is at one with the infinite. *(Darker)* At a certain point each day music plays. It seems to emanate from the very sun itself. Not so much a tune as a heartbreakingly beautiful vibration in the sunlight shining down on and through all the souls. A blanket of clear, almost unthinkable, harmonies. It's so moving you wonder how you could ever have doubted anything as you think back on this painful life which is just a sad distant memory. Time just slips away in heaven, Sharky. But not for you. No. You are about to find out that time is bigger and blacker and so much more boundless than you could ever have thought possible with your puny broken mind.

(Sharky looks down forlornly.)

Poor old Sharky. You've really got it for her, haven't you?

SHARKY: Who?

LOCKHART *(Derision)*: Who! The wife of that fella you were working for down in Lahinch.

(Sharky looks away.)

. . . That sent you all those CDs this morning! *(Derision)* "Who? . . ." Trust you to blow it, Sharky. Trust you. That's how I know you'll be coming with me tonight. I know you'll lose this next hand. Because you always make a pig's mickey of everything.

(Sharky seems to ponder his whole life for a moment, then goes to the bottle of poteen and pours himself a huge measure. He begins to drink it perfunctorily with one hand on his hip.)

That's it, Sharky, good man. Drink yourself up on to the next shelf in the basement. Drink to where possibility feels endless and your immortality feels strong.

(Sharky, having drained his glass, joylessly pours another.)

That's it . . . you poor stupid bastard.

SHARKY: Why don't you give it a rest?

LOCKHART: You nearly made it, Sharky. You were just two drinks away from never again!

SHARKY: I said give it rest.

LOCKHART *(Holding out his glass)*: Here, give me one.

SHARKY: Get it yourself.

LOCKHART: Oy, oy, oy! You listen to me. When you die, you go over a cliff so silently and the dusk swallows you so completely, you don't ever come back. You don't get another chance. You are gone.

SHARKY: So get your own drink.

(Sharky drinks while Lockhart looks at him, unsure for a moment. We hear a commotion as the others return to the kitchen through the back door. They are laughing.)

NICKY *(Wandering in to get a drink)*: They'd scarpered! They were gone!

RICHARD *(Coming through with Ivan)*: We chased them off! Another battle to us. The generals prevail! Ivan, would you please pour us a sharpener to warm us up? Mr. Lockhart? Are you all right for a . . . ?

LOCKHART: I don't know . . . This poor brain can't cope, I don't think!

RICHARD: Would you go on out of that? Have a stout! Ivan, are you all right? Ivan fell.

NICKY *(Laughs)*: Ivan wrecked himself!

IVAN: Ah, I walked right into that basin of dirty water Sharky left out there! Me socks are ringing!

RICHARD: You fucking eejit!

IVAN *(Going toward the kitchen)*: Ah, I'll take these off. I'll deal with it later . . .

RICHARD: You gobaloon . . . And, Sharky, what were you doing leaving a basin of water in the laneway? *(Imploring the heavens)* Lord, I'm surrounded by ninnies! Deliver me!

NICKY: Oh, I'll tell yous, Richard's blood is up!

RICHARD: What?

NICKY: He's missed his mill with the winos!

RICHARD: Excuse me?

NICKY: You were gunning for a fight so you were, go on out of that!

RICHARD: Yeah, right! Sure, how could I be? I'm blind, Nicky, actually, you know?

NICKY: Go on out of that! That never stopped you! *(Spies Sharky pouring a drink)* You having a Christmas nip, Sharky?

(Richard's ears prick up at this. Ivan falls in the kitchen trying to get his socks off.)

Wo! Easy there, Ivan! Are you all right?

IVAN: Yah . . .

RICHARD: So . . . Is Sharky back among the living, yeah?

LOCKHART: He's just trying to kill the pain.

RICHARD: Mr. Lockhart, take it from me: Sharky will never kill all that pain. He'd have to drink Lough Derg dry, God help him!

(They all laugh, except Sharky who continues to drink perfunctorily. Ivan wanders back in barefooted from the kitchen drinking a beer. Nicky brings Richard a drink.)

Ah, at last! Hey. Cheers, Sharky! *(Raises his glass, needling Sharky)* Welcome back!

(Sharky just looks at Richard darkly. Nicky, Ivan and Lockhart look at Sharky.)

SHARKY: Yeah. Cheers, Richard . . .

(Nicky and Ivan relax but . . .)

RICHARD: Ah, clink me glass, will ya?

(Sharky reluctantly goes and clinks his glass against Richard's.)

Good man. Drink up. Mr. Lockhart, it's a well-known fact in this whole area that my brother has that rare gift which is, unfortunately, the opposite to whatever the Midas touch was.

NICKY: Ah, Richard . . .

RICHARD: No, no . . . I'm going to say something positive. I believe that Sharky has potential. Yes. I believe he can change.

LOCKHART: Ah, well, that's sweet . . . Isn't that nice, Sharky?

NICKY: Yeah, lovely. Come on, are we gonna play cards? *(Sits at the table)*

RICHARD: You ever see an old couple going down the street, Mr. Lockhart? An old couple who've been married for a million years, going along the road to the shops or to mass, with their gray, dead faces?

LOCKHART: Yes.

RICHARD: Like some ghastly ancient brother and sister. Nothing to say to each other anymore or ever again except to snap the fucking head off each other for not putting the jelly back in the fridge or some fucking shite, you ever see that? Don't tell me they were always like that! Don't tell me they haven't *changed*! 'Cause I won't believe it! No, I believe in Sharky. He can change. I believe that he can change back to . . .

SHARKY: Back to what?

NICKY: Will I deal?

IVAN: Yeah go on, Nicky, deal . . .

LOCKHART: Hold on, Sharky wants to ask something . . .

RICHARD: What did you say?

SHARKY: Back to what? I can change back to what?

NICKY: Ah, lads . . .

RICHARD: Well . . . How about back to the little fella that always had a tune on his lips, and had integrity, and wasn't a sneaky little fucker who broke his mother's heart. How's that for starters?

NICKY: Ah, Richard, come on . . .

RICHARD: Back to that! You see, I remember, Mr. Lockhart, when it was all fields alls around here . . . all around all up to Donaghmede, all up to Sutton, all up to Howth. All fields, Mr. Lockhart. All farms, Nicky. Our mother was a wonderful woman! (*Suddenly stands up*) Our father was a fine man. A tough man. He was devoted to his greyhounds! He lived for them! Great with his fists.

LOCKHART: That's fascinating . . .

RICHARD: Yes. No, our mother, God rest her, she only ever had one problem in her life. Sharky. Yes . . .

NICKY: Ah, Richard, come on, that's the poteen talking. Sharky, sit down till we play . . .

RICHARD: He upset her that much, she hit him with a chair and broke it one night, Mr. Lockhart. I witnessed it.

NICKY: Ah, come on, Dick, come on, Sharky . . . let's not have the yearly . . .

SHARKY: What's your point, Richard?

RICHARD: Ha?

NICKY: Come on, Shark . . .

SHARKY: What? Did you want me to stay? And live here with you and them? And all the fucking rows all the time, and all the fucking drink?

RICHARD: You never needed anyone to show you how to drink!

SHARKY: 'Cause would you have got the house then?

RICHARD: What!

NICKY: Ah, lads, for fuck's sake . . .

LOCKHART: No, wait, let Sharky finish.

SHARKY: I am finished.

RICHARD: What do you mean would I have got the house then? How dare you?

SHARKY: You think you've always got it all figured out. Look at you.

RICHARD: What do you mean "look at me"? Look at you!!

SHARKY: Yeah well, don't worry about it. Because you know what? You're gonna get what you want.

NICKY: Ah, lads . . .

SHARKY: 'Cause I'm leaving here tonight and I'll be gone and that'll be the end of it.

(Sharky throws a chair across the room.)

NICKY: Ah, Sharky . . .

SHARKY *(Forcefully)*: And you can walk into the walls and spill
   Paddy Powers all down your horrible filthy whiskers and sit
   in your own stink 'cause you don't even know what day it is
   or what time it is. And then they'll stick you in some home
   out in Blanchardstown or somewhere where you won't even
   get a drink, how does that sound?

RICHARD: You're being completely unreasonable!

SHARKY: Am I? Just watch!

NICKY: Come on, Sharky, you don't mean it . . .

SHARKY: Yeah? Tell them, Mr. Lockhart, or whatever your fucking
   name is, go on, tell him! Tell him!

(Nicky is on his feet, trying to pacify Sharky.)

NICKY: Sharky . . . come on . . . it's all right . . .

SHARKY: Take your fucking hands off me, I'll give you such a box
   in the fucking head!

IVAN: Wo, wo . . . Sharky . . .

NICKY: Hey, easy, Shark . . .

SHARKY: You're only a fucking scumbag.

NICKY: What?

SHARKY: You heard me, you sponger.

(Ivan is also on his feet)

IVAN: Ah, Sharky, now, come on . . .

SHARKY: Eileen is far too good for a fucking scumhead like you.
   Always on the mooch . . .

NICKY: Hey! Don't be having a go at me! *(Rolls up his sleeve to show
   Sharky his tattoo)* Read that! What does that say! "Eileen"!
   And that? "Eileen"! I look after Eileen and the kids!

IVAN: Ah, lads!

NICKY: At least I don't be getting into mills all the time and getting barred out of pubs all over the place! At least I don't be waking up screaming and roaring at all hours of the night having bad dreams and freaking the kids out and waking the whole place up!

RICHARD: That's right!

SHARKY: What?

NICKY: Sure everybody knows! You're a nutcase, Sharky! Everybody knows!

(Sharky enters an inarticulate rage and throws a punch at Nicky. Nicky defends himself, pushing Sharky backward. Ivan manages to get a hold of Sharky and restrain him.)

RICHARD: What's going on? Sharky! Calm down!

(Sharky tries to escape Ivan's grip, dragging him over to Lockhart.)

SHARKY: Come on—you and me outside. Let's finish this, for once and for all!

IVAN: Come on, Sharky. Come on . . .

(Ivan bundles Sharky toward the kitchen.)

SHARKY *(Turns, shouting at Lockhart)*: You fucking bastard!

(Ivan gets Sharky into the kitchen and shuts the door. We hear Sharky's muffled cries for a moment and Ivan's soothing voice.)

LOCKHART: What did I do?

RICHARD: No, no, Mr. Lockhart, you didn't do anything. What did any of us do, sure? I can only say I'm terribly sorry . . . for his behavior . . .

LOCKHART: Not your fault, Richard.

NICKY *(Picking up an overturned chair and a glass)*: He's renowned for that temper. *Renowned* ... He can't drink! He never could! He's barred out of ... Richard?

RICHARD: Ah, he's barred out of nearly everywhere. He can't even get a job on the fishing boats anymore ... They won't have him.

NICKY: Yeah! Like, he had a go at all of us there! You know what I mean?

RICHARD: That's what I live with! That's what we all had to live with, with him.

(Nicky shakily pours them all a drink.)

If our poor old ma said left, Sharky said right. If our da said up, Sharky went down. They'd send him out on a message, maybe to get a few bottles of stout or whatever, he just wouldn't come back! He was like a stray cat in a sock, God help him. Always. And you also have to excuse that he hasn't had a drink in a couple of days, Mr. Lockhart. And I don't know why he bothers. That's like running into a brick wall at full tilt there now tonight again, the fucking eejit ... What's he drinking?

NICKY: He's drinking that fucking poteen shite you got from the north!

RICHARD: Yeah, I should have known ... But, this is the mad thing, he'll be grand now in a minute, watch! Won't he, Nicky?

NICKY: Oh yeah, he'll calm right down now, wait till you see ... I should probably be heading on soon anyway or we won't get a taxi ...

RICHARD: Ah, Nicky ...

NICKY: Fucking ... Sharky's left hook is nothing compared to Eileen's, I'll tell you!

RICHARD: She wouldn't hit you, Nicky ...

NICKY: It's the force of her words, Richard! Fucking pin you up against the wall ...

(They laugh. The kitchen door opens and a sheepish Sharky appears with Ivan. They are both holding cans of beer. Pause.)

SHARKY: I'm sorry, Nicky.
NICKY: Yeah, no worries, Shark . . .

(Pause.)

I'm sorry, Richard.
RICHARD *(Grandly)*: Apology accepted.

(They are silent. The wind continues to blow outside. Sharky stands near his chair. Nicky sits. Ivan sits.)

Are you not going to apologize to Mr. Lockhart?

(Pause.)

LOCKHART: No need. No need. No need.
RICHARD: No, Mr. Lockhart, I think he should—
LOCKHART: No, no! I perfectly understand. It was only the old drink talking. Sure I'm full of it myself. I'll tell you what: the only reparation I'd require, if no one objects is . . . let's all finish up like friends and play the last hand and we'll call it a night. How does that sound?
NICKY: Good idea!
IVAN: Ah, I don't know if maybe this is such a . . . *("good idea")*
NICKY: Yeah! It's all right for you there with a big pile of money in front of you!
RICHARD: No, no, don't worry, Nicky, we'll play, we'll play, won't we? Sharky? A last hand now, and no digs flying, all right?

(Pause.)

LOCKHART: Okay, Sharky?

SHARKY *(Looking at Lockhart)*: Okay . . .

RICHARD: Will someone pour Sharky a drink there, calm him down . . .

IVAN: He has one . . .

LOCKHART: Will I deal? *(Expertly shuffles the cards like a dealer in a casino)*

RICHARD: Fire away, Mr. Lockhart!

LOCKHART: I'll give 'em a good shuffle . . .

NICKY: You all right, Shark? *(Sharky nods)* I'm sorry as well, okay?

(Sharky nods, watching Lockhart shuffle. Nicky and Ivan put two euros each in the pot.)

RICHARD: He's grand! Leave him alone. I live with that silence!

LOCKHART *(Proffering deck to Sharky)*: Cut the deck, Sharky?

(A little pause before Sharky leans forward and taps the deck with his knuckle to indicate that he is satisfied with the cut.)

(Taking the cards and dealing) Right!

RICHARD: I feel a big win in me waters!

NICKY: That's my big win!

RICHARD: Then why am I feeling it in *my* waters?

NICKY: Your waters is warning you.

RICHARD: Oh, I don't know about that. I heard a little whistle from Santy down the chimney, Mr. Lockhart . . .

LOCKHART: Well, last hand! I feel something's really gonna happen . . .

NICKY: Something's got to give . . .

(They all collect their cards and peruse them.)

Well . . .

RICHARD: Anything interesting, Nicky?

NICKY: A card or two of note . . .

RICHARD: Ivan?

IVAN: We're doing all right . . .

LOCKHART: Care to open the betting, Ivan?

IVAN: Ah, last hand, we'll open it with five euros. *(Puts five euros in the pot)*

NICKY: Five euros?

RICHARD: Easy now, Ivan!

NICKY: Here, wait! Who's shy?

SHARKY: Oh sorry . . .

(Sharky puts two euros in the pot.)

LOCKHART: I'd hate for you not to be in this hand, Sharky.

SHARKY: Yeah . . .

RICHARD: So five to play, lads.

NICKY: I'll hang around. *(Puts in a fiver)*

LOCKHART: Sharky?

(Sharky considers.)

Ah, you're not gonna go without a fight?

RICHARD: Sharky's had more than enough fights! You should sit this one out, Shark, hang on to your few shekels and don't have me be bailing you out . . .

LOCKHART: Ah, it's the last hand . . .

RICHARD: Exactly!

SHARKY: No. I'm in. *(Puts in five and then throws in another note)* With twenty.

(The table reacts.)

RICHARD: With what? Twenty? You fucking berk!

NICKY: Ah, now, here! Hello . . .

RICHARD: What are you doing?

IVAN: Let him play, Rich . . .

RICHARD: Ah, this is mad! How are we doing? What have we got?

(Ivan leans over to confer with Richard, whispering in his ear.)

NICKY: God, Shark! I thought we were quits . . . the punishment continues!

LOCKHART: It's only a game!

NICKY *(Sarcastic)*: Oh *is* it?

LOCKHART: Are you in or out, Nicky?

NICKY: Ah fuck it, come on! *(Puts in twenty euros)*

LOCKHART: Ivan?

IVAN: We'll see it . . .

LOCKHART: And so will I.

(Ivan and Lockhart put in twenty.)

RICHARD: You're some bollocks, Sharky.

IVAN: Let him play, Dick.

LOCKHART: Ivan?

IVAN *(Throwing a card in)*: Just one please, Mr. Lockhart.

LOCKHART: One . . . *(Deals him a card)*

NICKY *(Incredulous)*: One?

RICHARD: Yes, Nicky, one.

LOCKHART: Sharky?

SHARKY: One.

NICKY *(Downbeat)*: One as well?

RICHARD: Ah, he's having a laugh, don't mind him.

NICKY: And what are yous doing?

RICHARD: We're not messing about. We're playing for keeps.

NICKY: Great . . . Give me three.

LOCKHART *(Dealing him three cards)*: Three.

(Nicky looks at his cards.)

RICHARD: That made you go quiet.

NICKY: Well . . .

RICHARD: What suddenly happened?

NICKY: No, nothing . . .

RICHARD: Go on out of that. Nicky suddenly has a hand.

NICKY: Why don't you play me and find out? With your pathetic little run up to a six or whatever it is.

RICHARD: Don't worry, we will. How many did you take, Mr. Lockhart?

LOCKHART: I'm happy.

NICKY: You're happy?!

LOCKHART: No cards. I'll stick with these.

NICKY: Oh bollocks.

LOCKHART: The bet's to Sharky.

RICHARD: Throw 'em in, Shark. Don't lose it all on a bluff now.

(Pause. Sharky considers Lockhart.)

SHARKY: Fifty.

NICKY: Oh God . . .

RICHARD: Sharky!

IVAN: No, let him play, Dick!

LOCKHART: Nicky?

NICKY: Oh God . . .

(Nicky gets up and walks away from the table.)

RICHARD: Where's he going?

NICKY: I'm thinking!

RICHARD: God help us!

(Pause. Nicky comes back, taking some money out of his pocket.)

NICKY: Come on! It's Christmas. Fifty. I'm in. And I'm fucked now.

LOCKHART: Ivan?

NICKY: Sure he *(Referring to Sharky)* has nothing.

IVAN: Yeah. *(Puts in fifty)*

RICHARD: Jaysus, you're very flathulach *(Irish for "generous")* with my money there now, Vano.

IVAN: Hey, I won some of this, too, Rich, don't forget.

RICHARD: Yeah well, easy come . . .

LOCKHART: And I'll see Sharky's fifty. With fifty.

NICKY *(Throws in his hand, stands up)*: Ah, here! If yous are . . .

RICHARD: With what?

IVAN: With fifty . . .

NICKY: 'Cause if yous are . . .

RICHARD: With fifty?!

IVAN *(Trying to keep Richard committed)*: No, hold on . . . hold on . . .

NICKY: This is just too expensive! I mean I can have fun for nothing, like!

RICHARD: You out, Nicky?

NICKY: I'm gone! I'm out . . . *(Goes and grabs his jacket; almost mumbling)* This is fucking crazy . . .

LOCKHART: Ivan?

(Ivan turns to whisper to Richard. Sharky sits watching Lockhart who returns his gaze.)

NICKY: Lads, I have to shoot. 'Cause we won't get a taxi . . .

RICHARD: Yeah, hold your horses . . .

NICKY: Yous have all me money!

RICHARD *(To Ivan)*: Go on, go on . . .

IVAN: We're in. *(Puts in fifty)*

NICKY: Jaysus . . .

LOCKHART: Sharky.

SHARKY: Here. *(Raising)* And whatever else this is . . . eighty . . .

LOCKHART: With eighty?

RICHARD: Sharky, what are you doing? You mad bollocks?

LOCKHART: Ivan?

NICKY: Lads . . . don't blow a good evening now . . .

IVAN: No, we'll see it . . .

RICHARD: Ivan . . .

IVAN: To you, Mr. Lockhart.

LOCKHART: Well, I've no change so I'll just throw in a hundred.

IVAN: So twenty to play. *(Puts in twenty to see the bet)*

RICHARD: Ivan!

IVAN: We're all right, Dick.

RICHARD: Speak for yourself!

LOCKHART: Sharky?

SHARKY: Em . . .

(Sharky stands up and searches his pockets. He pulls out some loose change.)

NICKY: Sharky's busted. You're gone, Shark, you're out . . .

LOCKHART: Well, if he wants to play . . . I know he's good for it.

RICHARD: Good for it?! He is not!

SHARKY: Richard, I have it.

RICHARD: Where? Under the mattress in Lahinch?

SHARKY: Yeah, just not . . . I have it.

RICHARD: Where?

NICKY: Ah, he's good for it, Rich.

LOCKHART: I'll play him.

RICHARD: What the fuck is this? Sharky, if we win, you've to cook that coddle I been asking you for, right?

SHARKY: Yeah, all right, I'll do it!

RICHARD: With the black pudding?

SHARKY: Yeah, all right!

NICKY: He'll do it . . .

RICHARD: Yeah, but what if Mr. Lockhart wins? Who's gonna pay him for Sharky?

SHARKY: I'll pay him myself.

RICHARD: With what?

IVAN: We'll give it to him!

RICHARD: We'll have fucking nothing left!

LOCKHART: We'll go up to the hole in the wall, sure. Isn't there one up there by the off-license?

RICHARD: The hole in the wall? *(Laughing)* Sharky has no bank account!

SHARKY: I have it, Rich, all right? Just let me play.

RICHARD: Do you have a sneaky bank account? Are you putting all my change from the shopping in there?

SHARKY: Would you give it a fucking rest?

RICHARD: You're gone mad!

LOCKHART: I'm happy to play him. I'm happy to go up to the hole in the wall if I win.

IVAN: Let him play, Rich . . .

RICHARD: Okay! But this is . . . I give up. I fucking give up!

LOCKHART: So? We're all in? Show our hands?

NICKY: Yous probably all have nothing have yous?

(Pause. Sharky takes a long drink.)

LOCKHART: Sharky?

SHARKY: I have a poker. Four eights.

(Sharky and Lockhart sit watching each other.)

NICKY: Four fucking eights? Bang!

IVAN: Yous are not gonna believe this . . .

RICHARD: I'm sick . . .

NICKY: What have you got, Ivan?

IVAN: We had a poker as well! Four fours!

RICHARD: Ah, this is a disaster!

NICKY: No!

IVAN: Four fours ... (*Throws his cards facedown with disgust*)

NICKY: Sharky wins! What a hand, though! Both of yous!

RICHARD: That is a total killer now ...

LOCKHART: Well, one moment, gentlemen, please ...

(*Pause. He lays his hand down for them to see. Sharky closes his eyes when he sees it.*)

NICKY: Four tens!!! What are the chances?!

RICHARD: What?

IVAN: Four tens ...

NICKY: Sharky ...

RICHARD: Did Sharky blow it?

NICKY: Sharky, you're beaten ...

RICHARD: Sharky, you fucking eejit!

NICKY: You had to play it.

RICHARD: What were you doing?

IVAN: He had to play with a hand like that, Dick, come on ...

RICHARD (*Angrily*): Ah!

NICKY: Well you certainly cleaned us all out, Mr. Lockhart.

LOCKHART: A pleasure, gentlemen ...

IVAN: Hard luck, lads ...

NICKY: Look I'm gonna have to see if I can grab a taxi. D'you want to share one, Mr. Lockhart?

LOCKHART (*Rising, collecting his money*): No, I'm going to walk, Nicky.

NICKY: All the way up to Howth?

LOCKHART: I always like to savor the last few hours in the dawn before the Child arrives. I never have too long you see.

NICKY (*Baffled*): Eh ... well ... whatever you want ... I'm gonna ... (*Zips up his jacket*)

LOCKHART: Sharky?

SHARKY: Yeah.

RICHARD: Here, take it from me, Mr. Lockhart, what do we owe you, twenty?

SHARKY: Nah, it's all right, Dick, I'll go with him . . .

RICHARD: But we have it here! Give it to me later!

SHARKY: Nah, I should give him my own . . . what I owe him.

RICHARD: Don't be ridiculous! It's the middle of the night!

SHARKY: No, it's fine. Really . . .

RICHARD: Talk about contrary! Sharky, come on . . .

NICKY: Here, Ivan, do you want a lift if I can grab a taxi out on the street?

IVAN: Oh, I don't know if I'd be welcome now at this hour . . .

NICKY: Would you not chance it? What time is it? It's a quarter to seven?! Oh bollocks!! How did that happen?

IVAN: What? Oh God, okay, let me have a slash quickly!

(Ivan jogs into the kitchen to use the toilet. Nicky runs up the stairs.)

NICKY: I'll see if I can grab a jo. I doubt it though . . . Bollocks! *(He is gone)*

LOCKHART: Well, Richard. It was very nice to make your acquaintance.

RICHARD: Yes! Well, thank you for calling.

LOCKHART: I hope you're not too sore about losing.

RICHARD: No, I'm just annoyed that I can't see and I can't play properly for myself. Or do anything that I'd really want. But we must do it again. Are you around?

LOCKHART: Oh, I'll be gone now . . . till Good Friday anyway.

RICHARD: Well, maybe around then. And please excuse my brother and his . . . behavior. Please, let me give you the twenty euros. I'm nervous about him going off out now at this hour . . . I just . . . he's had a few drinks and you've seen that he can be . . .

Sure, you'll nearly have to go all the way up to Sutton Cross! The cash machine at the shops has been empty for days now coming up to Christmas!

LOCKHART: I'd be happy to oblige you, Richard. But Sharky seems to feel he should pay me himself.

RICHARD (*Groping for money at the table, holding out what he has grabbed*): Jaysus, Sharky, I'll give it to you, all right? Happy Christmas, okay? Are you happy?

SHARKY: I have to go, Richard. I have to do it myself. I'm sorry.

RICHARD: Ah, I give up! Come straight back now, won't you?

(*Pause.*)

You promise me?

(*Short pause.*)

SHARKY: Yeah.

(*Nicky reappears, coming down the stairs.*)

NICKY: Where's Ivan? Is he coming? I have a jo! It's Mungo Mickey's brother, whathisname . . . He's on his way home, so come on! Ivan!

(*Ivan appears at the kitchen door wearing a big pair of spectacles.*)

IVAN: I found me glasses!

RICHARD: Well thank fuck for that!

NICKY: Come on, do you want to chance it, I'll bring you home?

IVAN: Oh, I don't know . . . I'm after really fucking blowing it now sure, it's the fucking morning!

RICHARD: Look, hang on here with me, Ivan, we'll give her a ring, all right? And smooth the passage . . .

IVAN: Yeah, maybe . . . Sure, I'm jarred, Nicky . . .

NICKY: Okay, well look, I'll see yous. Good luck, Richard.

(Nicky comes and shakes hands with Richard. Ivan sits at the table and takes a drink.)

RICHARD: See ya, Nicky, me old flower!

NICKY: And I'll be in to see you now over the Christmas. And we'll have a nice, proper *Christmas* drink . . .

RICHARD: Absolutely. You'll have to rescue me.

NICKY: Would you go on out of that, you don't need rescuing, Dick! *(Hurrying toward the stairs)* Lads, I'll see yous. You sure yous won't take a lift?

IVAN: Here, hold on . . .

(Ivan picks up his cards from the last hand.)

These is four aces!

NICKY: What? *(Goes to look)* It is! Yous had four aces, you dozy fucking eejit!

RICHARD: What's he saying?

NICKY: Yous had four aces!

IVAN: I thought they were fours, I couldn't . . .

NICKY: Yous won it! *(Turns to Lockhart)* They beat you, Mr. Lockhart . . .

LOCKHART: No . . .

NICKY: No, they did.

LOCKHART: Let me see . . .

(Nicky brings the cards to Lockhart.)

IVAN: I thought they were . . . you see I fucking thought they were fours! They were aces, see?

RICHARD: Well, happy Christmas!

IVAN: I just couldn't see them!

RICHARD: How many other hands did you balls up on me?

NICKY: Well, that saves you an auld trip to the hole in the wall, Sharky . . .

(Sharky and Lockhart look at each other.)

RICHARD: Let's have a drink! I *knew* that hand was ours! I could feel it in me waters! I told yous! Woo-hoo!

IVAN: I'm sorry about that, Mr. Lockhart . . .

NICKY: Oh, that's a pain in the hole, Mr. Lockhart. Lads, I have to run, I can't believe none of yous is coming with me! Come on, Mr. Lockhart, you might as well take a lift now . . . Come on!

(Lockhart stands there looking at them. Then he takes the money from his pocket and puts it on the table.)

LOCKHART: Well, what can I say? Somebody's done you a big favor, Sharky.

RICHARD: Hey, this is a square house, there's no cheating or favors being done when it comes to playing cards in here!

LOCKHART: I'm not saying it was anyone here . . .

RICHARD: What in the name of God are you talking about? It was just a mistake. People make mistakes, Mr. Lockhart. It's not the end of the world . . .

LOCKHART: No . . .

IVAN: I just couldn't see! They looked like fours . . . I didn't look at them properly, I'm sorry.

RICHARD: Hey, you owe *me* that twenty euros now, Sharky.

NICKY: Come on, Mr. Lockhart, I'll drop you at Sutton Cross, you can stroll up from there. Sharky. I'll see you, right?

SHARKY: Yeah. I'll see you, Nicky.

(Sharky and Nicky shake hands.)

NICKY: Call in over the Christmas, say hello, won't you?

SHARKY: Yeah.

NICKY: Good man. Ivan, I'll see you up in Doyle's no doubt. Have a good one, right?

IVAN: Yeah. Cheers, Nicky.

NICKY: And don't spend all that wonga until you get me a pint of Miller, or three, right? I'm gone! Come on, Mr. Lockhart, if we lose this lad we're goosed! *(Runs up the stairs)*

LOCKHART: Well then . . . I'll say good night.

RICHARD: Yeah, good morning! Happy Christmas! I hope Santy brings you what you want!

LOCKHART *(Buttoning up his coat)*: I only want what yous fellas have.

RICHARD: Yeah? What's that, then?

LOCKHART *(Putting on his hat)*: Peace of mind.

(Richard and Ivan burst out laughing.)

RICHARD: What? Are you fucking joking me?

LOCKHART: No. Good-bye, Richard. Good-bye, Ivan. See you again.

IVAN *(Pouring a drink for himself and Richard)*: Yeah, good luck.

LOCKHART: Good-bye, Sharky.

(Sharky doesn't answer him.)

Perhaps we'll play again some time, when my luck changes. Or yours does.

SHARKY: Nah, you're all right.

RICHARD: Sharky!

SHARKY: I just don't want to play anymore.

LOCKHART: Well you should think about it. Somebody up there likes you, Sharky. You've got it all.

(Lockhart unsteadily mounts the stairs and pauses at the window.)

How cold the moon always looks in the morning! So silent . . .

(Lockhart leaves. The light under the Sacred Heart blinks on. The first rays of dawn are seeping into the room. The front door slams.)

RICHARD: Well Jaysus! That is one maudlin fucker! Talk about a poor loser!

IVAN: Where do I know him from?

RICHARD: Ah, he's one of Nicky's strays. Jesus Christ, it's freezing in here!

SHARKY: Yeah, let me just . . . *(Goes to the stove and puts fuel in)*

RICHARD: Good man, Sharko! Hey do yous know what we should do? The monks do have an early mass in the friary. Do yous feel like it? Because then—this is brilliant—we'll get one of them to run you up home, Ivan, soothe Karen's temper and be an honest broker. How's that for genius?

IVAN *(Considers, not too convinced)*: Well, I don't know . . .

RICHARD: And you know of course that they brew their own ale up there? I was there when they started doling it out one Christmas. It's strong stuff. Two or three jugs of that after mass and you'll be whistling Dixie for the whole afternoon! What do you think, Sharky?

SHARKY: Yeah, I suppose we could walk up, if it's not still raining . . .

RICHARD: Hey, Sharky . . .

SHARKY: Yeah?

RICHARD: Go over to the tree.

SHARKY: What?

RICHARD: "What?" he says! What, did you think I didn't get you anything? What do you think I am? An ogre? Hey, Ivan, check out bah-humbug over here! Go on, Ivan, get yours as well. He knows what it is. He wrapped them for me, didn't you, Ivan?

(Ivan lets out a loud snore.)

SHARKY: He's having a nap.

RICHARD: Ah, leave him. Yours is there. It has your name on it. It doesn't matter. They're both the same.

SHARKY: Ah, Rich, are you serious?

RICHARD: Yeah, well you don't deserve it now after your disgraceful behavior. But sure, it's Christmas. All is forgiven. What do you say?

(Sharky goes to the tree and picks up one of the presents.)

Open it, you berk!

(Sharky tears the wrapping.)

You see what it is? It's a mobile phone!

SHARKY: Oh yeah. Thanks, Rich . . . it's . . .

RICHARD: Yeah well, that old 088 you were using, sure that's practically obsolete! No one can ever get you! I just thought that if you were gonna get back to the driving or if I ever needed to . . . that I could get you, you know . . .

SHARKY: Yeah . . . Thanks . . .

RICHARD: What? Is something wrong?

SHARKY: No, I'm . . . I'm just . . .

RICHARD: Ah, buck up will you, Sharky! I don't want the whole, *(A mocking, unfair impression of Sharky)* "Aw, life is too hard and I can't take it!" off you today now, right? Do you hear me? We all know you're an alcoholic and your life is in tatters and you're an awful fucking gobshite. We all know that. But you know what? You're alive, aren't you? *(Beat)* Aren't you?

SHARKY: Yeah.

RICHARD: So come on! Buck up now! It's Christmas day and I feel like going to mass, so go on and put the kettle on! Ivan!

(Ivan jumps.)

IVAN: What?

RICHARD: You better get a cup of tea into you. Come on, we're gonna go up to mass. And see if we can get one of the monks to broker a peace deal for you. *(Going toward the stairs)* Hey, Shark, do I have a clean shirt?

SHARKY: I left one on your bed.

RICHARD: Good man, stick on a bit of toast will you? Ivan, you might come up and help me get a shave in a minute, is that all right?

IVAN: Yeah, no problem, Dick.

RICHARD *(Going up)*: Hey, lads, we really showed that fucker didn't we?

IVAN: We sure did.

RICHARD: There was a funny smell off him. Get Ivan a bit of breakfast, will you, Sharky?

SHARKY: Do you want a bit of toast, Ivan?

IVAN: Oh, I don't think so . . . I don't think I'm quite there yet.

SHARKY: Well I'll put the kettle on. *(Goes to the kitchen)*

RICHARD *(As he disappears)*: Good man, Sharky. That's the way.

(Ivan wanders over to the stereo. He takes a CD from Sharky's gift box. Morning is really beginning to pour in now. The wind has died down. The sky is clear.)

IVAN: Hey, Shark! She has good taste, your one who sent you these . . .

(Sharky comes out with a tray, tidying up.)

SHARKY: What's that?

IVAN: No, I said you got some good music off your friend down the country.

SHARKY: Yeah?

IVAN: Yeah. These are classics.

SHARKY: Stick one on.

IVAN: Will I?

SHARKY: Yeah go on . . .

(Sharky continues to tidy up while Ivan puts on a CD. John Martyn's "Sweet Little Mystery" begins to play softly. Ivan stands nodding his approval in time with the music, then goes up the stairs to help Richard. Sharky pauses for a moment. He reaches into his pocket and takes out the gift card. He stands there reading, as John Martyn sings: "It's not the letters that you just don't write / It's not the arms of some new friend / It's not the crying in the depth of the night / That keeps me hanging on / Just waiting for the end . . ." The sunlight seems to stream in brighter and brighter for a moment, before it fades away with the music.)

END OF PLAY